HORATIO'S VERSION

Horatio's Version

by
ALETHEA HAYTER

FABER & FABER
3 Queen Square London

First published in 1972
by Faber and Faber Limited
3 Queen Square London WC1
Printed in Great Britain by
Latimer Trend & Co Ltd Plymouth

ISBN 0 571 09851 7

Preface

Shakespearean scholars have forbidden us to guess at the number of Lady Macbeth's children. Shakespeare's characters, they remind us, have no existence outside the plays in which they appear. Dover Wilson, for instance, writes: "Critics who speculate upon what Hamlet was like before the play opens, who talk about his life with Horatio at Wittenberg, discuss how he came to fall in love with Ophelia, or attribute his conduct to a mother-complex acquired in infancy, are merely cutting the figure out of the canvas and sticking it in a doll's-house of their own invention. . . . Verisimilitude and not consistency or historical accuracy is the business of drama. . . . Horatio is not a person in actual life or a character in a novel but a piece of dramatic structure".

The scholars themselves do not always succeed in practising this hard doctrine which they preach. C. S. Lewis, setting out to show how the nineteenth-century character criticism of Shakespeare's plays for a long time hampered his appreciation of them, and insisting that all conceptions of the characters reached by working out what sort of a man it would be who in real life would act and speak as they do, are chimerical, nevertheless lets fall that "the affection we feel for the Prince, and through him, for Horatio, is like a friendship in real life".

For the rest of us, not scholars but ordinary members of the audience, the doctrine is more than hard—it is impossible. These people, these characters of Shakespeare's, are our lifelong companions, more real to us—more likely to be turned to for comfort or amusement or example—than many of the living people that we know or have read about in the newspapers. Benedick, Viola, Mercutio, Hector, Desdemona, Kent, are loved and admired friends; Cleopatra, Henry V, Prospero, the Venetian merchant Antonio, are endless subjects of curiosity. We like to gossip about them, to pry into their affairs. It is no use telling us that they have no existence outside the action of the plays in which they appear. They exist in our imaginations; and what goes on there, as long as it does not pass itself off as scholarship or literary criticism, is free.

This work of mine is therefore not for Shakespeare scholars, or for professional producers of Shakespeare's plays, who are now interested in their political message or their symbolism, not in their events and characters. This book is a game for the audience, for the ordinary theatre-goer who has argued in the bar during the entr'acte whether Angelo and Mariana settled down in the moated grange after their marriage, or whether Edmund's mother murdered Edgar's, or whether Lysander's wealthy dowager aunt would really have cared much for Hermia. To those who fear that this kind of game may distract the audience from the real splendours and miseries of the plays, I would suggest that attention is a habit, not a quantity; the harder you look, for any reason, the more you see. Granville-Barker, pondering why Claudius didn't let Hamlet go back to Wittenberg, remarked that no modern audience would ask this question, but added "If only they *would* ask questions about this play they think they know so well, how much more they would enjoy it!"

In this reconstruction of events after the close of *Hamlet*, I have not invented any characters; all those who appear are from the play itself. Practically all the evidence given at the Court of Enquiry is shown in the play to have been seen by, or known to, the survivors who give evidence, or could reasonably have been deduced by them from what they knew already. I have gone nearest to invention in the evidence given on the final day of the Enquiry, but it is obvious that some piece of villainy, not mentioned in the text of the play, is implied by the discrepancy between Act IV Scene vii 165–82 and Act V Scene i 1–30. If any Shakespeare expert should after all read this book, he will see that I have in the main followed the stage directions and notes in Dover Wilson's Cambridge edition, and his arguments in *What Happens in Hamlet*, though I venture to differ from him on several points. My conjectures as to what the original version of the play *The Murder of Gonzago* may have been like, before Hamlet's alterations to it, are more fully developed in an article which appears in the January 1972 number of *Ariel*.

This is Horatio's version and, like him, is limited to the practical straightforward side of the Elsinore events, and it is related in the common-sense style which he would have used. No attempt is made to fathom or explain the psychology and motives of Hamlet and Claudius further than these would have been understood by Horatio. Horatio was sensible and well educated, kind and brave; he was not an intellectual, nor had he much subtlety, and it is evident that much of what happened passed over his head. He saw the actual events and he knew what Hamlet had told him. He was a man of independent moral judgment, believing in Divine Providence but little given to imaginative speculation on religious truths or the after-life, though he had clearly read the standard textbooks. He judged everyone's actions, even Hamlet's, by a set of moral values based on ordinary human decency. No one was exempt from this standard, but his kindness and sympathy enabled him to see that even such abject creatures as Rosencrantz and Guildenstern deserved some pity.

Most middle-brow theatre-goers probably react to the events of the play much as Horatio does. Perhaps, indeed, Shakespeare put Horatio into the play to stand for the audience. Like him, they sympathize with Hamlet without understanding him or approving of all his actions. I am one of them, and to those of my fellow theatre-goers who, like me, are also fond of detective stories, I dedicate *Horatio's Version*.

Brussels, December 1970

Witnesses, in Order of Appearance

Francisco, a Soldier

A Norwegian Captain

Horatio, Friend to Hamlet

Osric, a Courtier

First Gentleman

Lady-in-Waiting

Lord-in-Waiting

First Switzer

Second Switzer

First Player

English Ambassador

Bernardo ⎫
Marcellus ⎬ officers

Priest

Reynaldo, Servant to Polonius

Chairman of the Enquiry

Voltimand, a Courtier

Extracts from a Diary

The new King has decided that the facts had better be made clear by a public enquiry, with witnesses. I told him that the Prince had asked me to tell the true story to him and to the people, but he has made up his mind that it would be safer for it to be all brought out in this way by a regular enquiry—safer for him, he means. I can see his point; although he was properly elected to the throne—in fact, there was no other possible candidate left, and I told the Council of State that the Prince had voted for him—still he knows that the people are restive, and there are a lot of rumours.

But I wish he had let me just stand up and tell everyone the essential facts, so that the world and posterity would know what really happened. Now that it's going to be done in this way, it will be hard to decide how much to tell and what to leave out. I can't explain how it all started, I'm bound by that terrible oath not to reveal that. And I think the Prince would have wanted me to keep the women out of it, however much they were implicated or made tools of. Then there's the voyage to England—it would be better not to bring in that part of the story, it cuts both ways, though I've got one vital piece of evidence there that I may have to use.

Voltimand is to be Chairman of the Enquiry. It would have been better to have had somebody completely indepen-dent. Voltimand backed the usurper and the marriage. Still, he was away in Norway as an ambassador for part of the time, and he wasn't at Court even after he got back, except for that one day when he reported on his mission and Claudius gave a banquet for him and Cornelius. He's a capable ambassador, probably he will be a business-like Chairman of the Enquiry.

I suppose he will call me as the first witness. Who else can he be going to call? Osric, perhaps. No doubt Osric will try and twist things to make them look a bit less damning for the other side, but he can't deny what actually happened, there are too many people left who were there and saw it, there must have been at least a dozen of us.

It would be better if someone else, someone good at making speeches, could tell the story to the Court of Enquiry. It will have to be me, though. Somehow I must make it clear, so that they'll see the real truth. It's the only thing left that I can do for him. It was to get the true story told that he stopped me killing myself. No, it wasn't only for that, he said that because he knew it would stop me. He wanted to save my life. What sort of a life did he think would be left for me?

The Romans thought a man had a right to kill himself. The Church calls it self-slaughter, but the Stoics thought it was justifiable. Cato killed himself. That was to save his honour, though, to be loyal to an idea. But there were others —there was Seneca; but he had no choice in the end. Did he feel the same then, when it came to the point, as what he'd written before as a general maxim? How does it go—*Patet exitus; si pugnare non vultis, licet fugere; quis vos tenet invitos*? "If you don't want to fight": that's the crux. For a man to kill himself, not to escape dishonour or disgrace, not because he's in prison or has got cancer, but in order to free himself from grief—perhaps it is running away from the fight. If he's mad, beside himself, that's different. No one would blame that poor crazy girl Ophelia. For a sane man—I don't know, now. At the time, I didn't have the least doubt, I

14

didn't even decide, I just knew it was what I would do, like a Roman. That may come back. What's that other tag of Seneca's, I've heard the Prince quote it: *Puncto securitas constat*. A pin-prick—yes. Not poison again, just one stab. But I must get this Enquiry over first.

Proceedings of a Court of Enquiry

HELD AT ELSINORE,
UNDER THE CHAIRMANSHIP OF VOLTIMAND,
DANISH AMBASSADOR TO NORWAY

First Day, First Session

(The Chairman opened the proceedings by announcing that
he had been commanded by King Fortinbras, who had just
acceded to the Throne of Denmark, to conduct an enquiry
into the deaths of the late King Claudius and Queen Gertrude, of Prince Hamlet, and of Laertes, son of the late
Chancellor Polonius. King Fortinbras was most anxious that
the whole truth about this very distressing affair should be
fully established, and had therefore decided that all surviving
witnesses of the terrible events of August 28th should be
called to give evidence as to what had occurred. The Chairman would begin by calling two witnesses who would describe the condition of the corpses as found. He ordered the
first witness, Francisco, to take the stand).

FRANCISCO: I am a sergeant in the Palace Guard. On Tuesday
of last week I was on duty on the ramparts when I was
ordered to go to the Great Hall with a squad to remove
some corpses up to the platform. The new King
changed his mind afterwards, and had the bodies put
elsewhere, but those were the orders at first.
VOLTIMAND: Will you tell the Enquiry how you found the
bodies disposed in the Great Hall when you got there?
FRANCISCO: The Queen was lying half on the ground, but
with her head and arms on one of the thrones. She was
the worst—her face was a dark colour and her eyes
staring—it made you feel sick, having to handle the

body. King Claudius was lying on his face, he must have knocked over the table as he fell, he was all among the flagons with wine spilling out of them, and a lot of blood round him too. Laertes was on his back, a bit blood-stained about the chest too, but not like the King. Prince Hamlet didn't look as bad as the rest, his body was leaning back against the dais, more in a peaceful sort of way.

VOLTIMAND: You knew nothing about what had happened till you were summoned to remove the bodies?

FRANCISCO: Nothing at all. I was on guard up on the ramparts, as I said. I'd had an order earlier on from King Claudius about firing a salute, but otherwise I heard nothing about what was going on.

(The Chairman explained that the next witness, though not a Danish subject, had been called to give evidence because immediately after the removal of the bodies he had been instructed by King Fortinbras to examine them and if possible establish the cause of death. His evidence would be the only report available as to the condition of the bodies after the event, since in the very understandable confusion at the time, the instructions that an autopsy should be performed did not reach the Court doctor till the interments had already taken place. The Chairman therefore asked the witness to explain how he came to examine the bodies, and what conclusions he had reached).

CAPTAIN: I am a Captain in the Norwegian Expeditionary Force which campaigned in Poland this summer. I was A.D.C. to King Fortinbras when he reached Elsinore on his way back last week, and when he heard what had happened here, he told me to examine the bodies; he knew I'd had a good deal of experience with wounds and injuries.

VOLTIMAND: I was informed when I was in Norway in May that the Expeditionary Force had only been recruited fairly recently, and the campaign in Poland was quite a short one. Where did you gain the experience of which you speak?

CAPTAIN: I wasn't born the day I joined Fortinbras's army. I was a mercenary before that.

VOLTIMAND: You should say "His Majesty" or "King Fortinbras".

CAPTAIN: Sorry. He wasn't a King when I joined up.

VOLTIMAND: Very well. Describe the injuries on the bodies which you examined.

CAPTAIN: I first examined the body of a rather bloated man of about fifty who I was told was King Claudius. He had been stabbed through the chest with some weapon like a rapier. It was a nasty wound and there must have been a lot of blood. The rapier missed his heart, but the wound would probably have killed him fairly soon unless it had been stanched.

VOLTIMAND: You say "would probably have killed him". Was there some other cause of death, then?

CAPTAIN: There may have been some other contributory cause. He was bruised about the mouth, but he may have got that in falling—I understood he was found lying on his face, and with his weight he would have fallen heavily.

VOLTIMAND: The Prince and Laertes presumably died of their wounds?

CAPTAIN: I was puzzled about that. The young man who I was told was Laertes was wounded in the right side, seriously but again, I'd have said, not badly enough to have caused death within a few minutes, as I gather it did. Prince Hamlet's wound was very slight, just a graze in the upper part of his left arm, apparently given him from behind.

(At this point Horatio intervened to say that he would be able to explain all this in the evidence that he would be giving. The Chairman asked him not to speak at this stage, and turning to the witness, asked whether he was positive that none of the wounds described could have caused death).

CAPTAIN: Almost impossible in Prince Hamlet's case, I'd say. I couldn't be positive about the other two. The King must have been in poor condition; I take it he was a heavy drinker; that might have made a wound mortal to him which wouldn't have been to another man.

VOLTIMAND: Would you say the same applied to Prince Hamlet?

CAPTAIN: Not enough to account for his dying of such a slight wound. I only saw him once alive—he exchanged a few words with me when he was on the way to England and we were marching to Poland—and he certainly looked pale then, but he wasn't overweight like his uncle.

VOLTIMAND: Is there any indication which of the deaths took place first?

(Here Horatio again attempted to intervene, but was told by the Chairman that he must wait his turn; he would be given full opportunity later to give his version of the events. The Chairman called on the Captain to continue with his evidence).

CAPTAIN: You couldn't really tell much about that from the state of the bodies. I was told when I was called to look at them that all the deaths had happened shortly before. There were some slight signs that Prince Hamlet died last of the four, and the Queen first, but that's only a guess.

VOLTIMAND: Did you reach any conclusion as to the cause of

the Queen's death? There was no wound in her case, was there?

CAPTAIN: No. The state her face and eyes were in suggested some form of poison, but I don't know much about poisons. I'm a soldier, not a doctor. I've told you what I actually observed, and how it squared up with wounds I'd seen before, but that's where I stop.

(The Chairman then said that this was clearly a very confused as well as a very terrible affair. He would recapitulate the evidence so far. In the Queen's case the cause of death was uncertain, but might have been poison, whether administered by herself or by some other person was not clear. The King and Laertes had apparently died of wounds, though this was not clear either. Prince Hamlet, as the last survivor, could in theory have killed the other three, and then committed suicide, but the position of his wound ruled out its being self-inflicted, and it was in any case too slight to have caused death. He hoped that the surviving witnesses of this shocking catastrophe would be able to make the order of events clearer. The Enquiry would now adjourn for two hours, after which he would call Prince Hamlet's friend Horatio).

Diary

(continued)

This Voltimand was the man who I believed would be a "business-like Chairman". It's plain now that he's one of those officials who must keep to their own rules which they've fixed in advance, no matter how badly they work. He's muddled the story altogether with these guesses by outsiders about events which could have been reported without mystery by the people who were actually there. Was I right to try and interrupt, though? It will have made the public realize they weren't hearing the real story, but it irritated Voltimand. If I've offended him, it may do harm. Why did he drag in that bit at the end about its being theoretically possible for the Prince to have killed all the others? Has someone been getting at him?

I must not let my misery and resentment make me suspicious. I must remember what happened to Coriolanus. He missed the consulship because he lost his temper over vexatious formalities. Voltimand is very like the Roman tribunes who wouldn't let Coriolanus off any of the traditional forms. I will think of that, and take it easy. God knows I'm not at all like Coriolanus, anyway. I'm just a mouthpiece for the truth.

After all, it doesn't really matter what muddle they made this morning. I shall be able to tell the true story later today when the Court of Enquiry meets again.

Court of Enquiry Proceedings

First Day, Second Session

(The Chairman reopened the session and called on Horatio to describe the events of 28th August, but first to state his nationality and position).

HORATIO: I am Danish, but have spent much of my life abroad. Up to this year I have been a student at the University of Wittenberg, but when I returned to Denmark for the late King Hamlet's funeral, I intended to look for a job.

VOLTIMAND: You have no family or estate in Denmark?

HORATIO: No. My parents are dead, and I have no private means.

VOLTIMAND: I understand you were a friend of Prince Hamlet?

HORATIO: Yes. We met at Wittenberg, where the Prince was also a student.

VOLTIMAND: No doubt the Prince would have secured a place at Court for you.

HORATIO: I expect he would have done if I had asked him to, but I didn't. When I came back to Denmark for the funeral, I got in touch with some friends of mine in the Palace Guard, Captain Marcellus and Lieutenant Bernardo, as I had some idea of joining the Palace Guard myself. I'd heard rumours that there might be a war with Norway before long. But it was then that . . .

VOLTIMAND: Thank you, that answers my question about your personal standing. I will now ask you to give us as full an account as possible of the events of August 28th.

HORATIO: I hope you will allow me to start the story rather earlier on, as it will be hard to explain how it all ended without telling you what led up to it.

VOLTIMAND: That would carry us too far afield, into matters with which this Enquiry is not concerned. I must ask you to confine yourself to the events of the day in question.

(The witness here paused for some time, but presently resumed his evidence).

HORATIO: Very well, Sir. That morning the Prince and I were talking in the Great Hall when Osric brought a message from King Claudius that he had put a bet on a fencing-match between the Prince and Laertes. The Prince agreed to take on the match straight away, and King Claudius and Queen Gertrude and some members of the Court arrived to watch it. The foils for the fencing-match were put on a table at one side of the hall, and the Prince took one without examining the others. The King announced that he would present a jewel as a prize to the winner. The match started, and the Prince scored a hit in the first bout. The King then drank to his health, and a salute was fired; the King's winecup was filled again, the King put the prize pearl into it, and proffered it to the Prince, who said that he would play the next bout first, before drinking. He scored in the next bout, too, and the Queen took up the cup with the pearl in it, and drank a toast to wish the Prince good luck. The King tried to stop her, but he wasn't in time.

(Voices in Court: "No!", "That's wrong". The Chairman called for silence, and told the witness to proceed).

HORATIO: The Prince and Laertes fought a third bout, in which neither of them scored, but just after the Prince had lowered his rapier at the end of the bout, and turned away, Laertes suddenly shouted something and lunged, and gave the Prince a slight wound in the arm.

OSRIC: I protest most, but most emphatically; that was during the bout, not after.

(The Chairman told Osric that he would be called later, but must be silent now).

HORATIO: The Prince realized at once that Laertes's rapier must have been unbated, or it wouldn't have wounded him, so he attacked Laertes and got hold of his rapier, letting Laertes pick up the other one. He then got through Laertes's guard with a quick pass, and wounded him in the side.

(Voices in Court: "What?", "No!". The Chairman said that he must have silence in Court or he would have it cleared. He told the witness to proceed).

HORATIO: The King shouted to the umpires and the Switzer guard to part the Prince and Laertes, but in fact they had already stopped fighting because Laertes's wound had incapacitated him. Just then the Queen suddenly collapsed, and screamed out something about the drink being poisoned. The Prince called for the door to be locked; he saw at once that there had been treachery, and Laertes . . .

VOLTIMAND: Was the door locked? This might be very important for the evidence as to who was present.

HORATIO: Yes, I secured it myself, but I think one of the Switzer guards had rushed out first, I suppose he went to turn out the rest of the Guard for a search when Prince Hamlet called out that there had been treachery. Laertes then confessed that his rapier had been unbated, and that both it and the cup that the Queen drank from had been poisoned. He said that the Prince had only half an hour to live after the wound given to him, and that the King was to blame . . .

(Tumult in Court, voices crying "Shame!", "Who?", "Did he say that?". The First Gentleman of the Royal Household rose and demanded to be heard).

FIRST GENTLEMAN: I must lodge a formal protest now against the farrago of untruths which we have just heard. I shall claim the right to give evidence later, but I cannot let these malicious and lying statements pass without protest.

VOLTIMAND: I must confess that I myself have been extremely surprised by this witness's allegations, and he will certainly be required to substantiate them. But I must insist that he should be allowed to finish his story without further interruption.

HORATIO: I am just as surprised at the protests by Osric and King Claudius's Gentleman. Everyone else who was there will certainly be able to confirm my account of what happened. I can understand that mistaken loyalties to their dead friends should induce these two gentlemen to deny what actually happened . . .

OSRIC: It couldn't by any tiny chance be a case of your mistaken loyalty to your dead friend, could it?

VOLTIMAND: These interruptions are most improper on both sides. The witness will continue, but must confine himself to an account of what took place, without any observations about possible motives.

HORATIO: When the Prince realized that King Claudius had plotted his death, both by the poisoned drink and the conspiracy with Laertes over the poisoned sword . . .

VOLTIMAND: I have warned you that you must not attribute motives in this way. No, I cannot allow further protests from others present. The witness will continue.

HORATIO: I am not guessing at the Prince's motives. His own words, heard by all those present, confirmed that he stabbed the King, and forced him to drink from the poisoned cup, because of what Laertes had just revealed. After the King's death, the Prince and Laertes exchanged forgiveness, just before Laertes died too. Then the Prince turned faint. He had time to ask me to tell the full and true story, as I am doing now, and then, in a little time, he died.

(The Chairman then said that this was obviously an even more difficult and distressing affair than had been supposed. They had heard descriptions of violent actions, and suggestions had been made which were even more shocking than the actions themselves. It was clear that the most thorough enquiries would have to be made. All those who had been present would be questioned most carefully and searchingly, so that all the facts could be brought to light. He hoped that the members of the public who were present in Court would refrain meanwhile from starting any more rumours or speculations. There had already been far too many of these. As patriotic Danes, they must all want to see settled conditions return to the country as soon as possible, and he therefore appealed to their loyalty and good sense to preserve order and to co-operate to the full in discovering the truth. The Enquiry would now adjourn till tomorrow, when the other witnesses to the catastrophe would be called to give their evidence).

Diary

(continued)

I have been on the ramparts with Marcellus and Bernardo, talking things over. We were there a long time, walking along the battlements by the sea. It's overcast tonight, and hot—very different from that frosty night in May when it all started out there on the battlements. There was a break in the clouds a good way out to sea, you could see the swell, great smooth heaving waves, and the moonlight glistening on them like oil.

Marcellus and Bernardo were astonished at what I'd revealed at the Enquiry today, about Claudius's plots against Hamlet. But they're both entirely on the Prince's side. They had suspected, of course, that something wicked was at work, ever since they saw the Ghost. But Bernardo said he thought it appeared as a warning of some horrible danger from Norway, something it was desperate to reveal; he didn't suspect it had anything to do with Claudius. Marcellus knew it had a special message for Hamlet, but that was all. Bernardo said he wished the Ghost would appear at the Enquiry—that would frighten Osric and his friends into telling the truth.

We can make jokes about the Ghost now, but we were all afraid when we actually saw it. It's no good thinking about that. Speculations of that kind can do no good, they only make you morbid. It set us talking about the old King when he was alive, though. I only saw him that once, but the others knew him well by sight. He was splendid to look at, and they said he could be kind and gracious, but terrible when he was angry, he'd done some ferocious things. He was astonishingly brave, of course. When Marcellus first told me they'd seen the

Ghost, I went and looked at the battle pictures of King Hamlet in the lobby. The best are the ones of his duel with old Fortinbras and of his battle with the Poles on the frozen river. A fine face, but a stern one. And yet the Prince loved him. I suppose he may have been different with his own family. He was open and unsuspicious, too, Hamlet would have liked that. Nothing like as clever as his son, though. The Prince was really more like his uncle than his father in that way—in natural power of mind, I mean, not in the use he made of it, God knows.

I reminded Marcellus and Bernardo that they mustn't mention the Ghost's appearances to anyone. Marcellus entirely agreed, but Bernardo was inclined to question it, till I said that it wouldn't be necessary anyway. Whatever Osric says at the Enquiry tomorrow, the evidence of the rest will confirm my story.

How ridiculous Osric looked today, popping up to protest in that fantastic hat, "most, but most emphatically". He's capable of spite, all the same, and Hamlet did make fun of him that day, I could see he resented it. I egged the Prince on, too, it was just as much my fault.

I suppose it's not surprising anyway that Osric wants to defend Laertes's memory. He admired Laertes tremendously, he couldn't stop talking about him when we were arranging about the fencing-match. It's rather pathetic in a way that such a midget as Osric should want to model himself on a tough athletic man like Laertes.

I can't condemn Laertes altogether, even now. He was treacherous, but he had cause for resentment, and he did repent at the end. That last exchange between them is a good thing to remember. It would have been even worse than it was if they'd both died unreconciled after that horrible scuffle by Ophelia's grave at the funeral. Hamlet saw almost at once how unworthy all that business was, but I was afraid Laertes was

28

too much of an egoist to meet Hamlet any part of the way. Osric ought to see that the best thing he can do for Laertes's memory is to tell everyone what Laertes's last words to Hamlet were.

It's odd that that First Gentleman of Claudius's should have tried to cast doubt on my story too. What has he got to gain by it? They were all terrified of Claudius in his lifetime, and agreed with every word that he said, but now that Claudius is dead, there seems no advantage in it for him. Not that it will matter very much if he denies that Laertes said what he did. There are the other witnesses, and no one can explain away the Queen's death, or Hamlet's own. In a way it is a good thing that Osric and the Gentleman took the line they did. It has forced Voltimand to say that I must substantiate my accusation of Claudius, and that will give me the chance to tell everybody that he murdered his brother. I meant to start with that, if Voltimand had let me tell the whole story in the order it happened. But as things turned out, it may be better that I couldn't bring it into my evidence today. It will strike all the world much more when they hear it by itself, as the reason for everything that Hamlet did.

I have been trying to work out who the witnesses tomorrow are likely to be. Who exactly was in the Great Hall that day? I must try to visualize the procession coming into the hall before the fencing-match. Claudius and the Queen first; Laertes, Osric, the First Gentleman who tried to give me the lie at the Enquiry today—he was the other umpire at the match, besides Osric. That old Lord-in-Waiting of Claudius's was there, and there must have been a Lady-in-Waiting too. Rather surprisingly few members of the Court, now I come to add up who was there; I suppose Claudius didn't want too many witnesses for what he'd planned to do. There were some Switzers of his bodyguard, I think. There must have been someone with a drum, I remember hearing it. Some servants brought in the table and the wine and the rapiers. Did they stay? I don't remember that. It's not such a crowd as I thought it had been, but still, quite enough to back up my story. I will send a word to the old Lord, and arrange to see him tomorrow morning before the Enquiry opens. Marcellus said he would get hold of that sergeant tonight to see if he could tell us any more than he said at the Enquiry today.

Later. Francisco came, but he couldn't add anything to what he had already said, except that it was one of the Switzers who brought him the orders about the gun-salute. I asked if he could find the Switzers who were on duty that night, and send them for a word with me. But he says the Switzers are a quite independent unit, recruited by Claudius as his own body-guard; they don't come under the Palace Guard, and the two units don't have much to do with each other. "No use my trying to round them up for you, Sir" he said; "they'd just turn awkward, as likely as not". I asked him whether any of his men had been down in the City this evening when they were off duty, and had heard any rumours or reactions. He said they'd heard everyone saying they were very sorry about Hamlet's death, and wishing he'd survived to succeed Claudius as King. I asked what people thought about what has come out at the Enquiry, but he didn't seem to have gathered anything about that—it's too soon for word to have gone round yet, I suppose. It has cheered me a little to hear that the people still feel like that about the Prince.

Court of Enquiry Proceedings
Second Day, First Session

(The Chairman said that he would now call all the other witnesses who had been present at the events on August 28th. He must remind them all that they should confine themselves to saying what they had actually seen and heard, and should not indulge in any theories or general observations. He would now call on the First Gentleman of the late King Claudius to take the stand).

FIRST GENTLEMAN: I am First Gentleman of the Royal Household. I was present throughout the events which are the subject of this Enquiry, and though I will of course bow to the Chairman's ruling about general observations, I shall find it impossible to conceal my astonishment and concern at the very misleading account of those events which we heard yesterday. I was actually one of the two umpires at the fencing-match, and I was therefore bound to pay particular attention to all that went on.

VOLTIMAND: In that case your evidence about what happened towards the end of the match will be particularly important. Pray proceed.

FIRST GENTLEMAN: There were three quite normal bouts. Prince Hamlet scored once in each of the first two. My impression was that Laertes, who was certainly the better swordsman of the two, allowed the Prince to score out of politeness, and to please the King and Queen. The King had offered a handsome prize to the winner, and naturally he would have preferred it to go to his nephew. Laertes

31

tactfully allowed this to happen, but he scored a hit in the third bout, so as not to let the Prince think he was being allowed a walk-over.

HORATIO: It wasn't during the bout, it was afterwards in the break, when the Prince had turned away.

VOLTIMAND: I must remind you that yesterday, when you were giving evidence and there were interruptions, I overruled them so that you could continue your story. Today it is your turn to listen in silence. If you interrupt again, you will be asked to leave the Court. The witness will proceed.

FIRST GENTLEMAN: As I was saying, Laertes scored a hit in the third bout. For some reason, this seemed to make Prince Hamlet furious—he didn't like losing, I suppose. He suddenly rushed at Laertes and wrestled with him, and then drew a dagger and stabbed him. He seemed to go berserk. We'd all been expecting, ever since he murdered Polonius, that he would break out again, but this was so sudden that we were all stunned. The Queen actually fainted at the sight of Laertes's blood, and that made the Prince still more beside himself, and before we could do anything he suddenly shouted and leapt on the King and stabbed him. It was an appalling attack of homicidal mania—it is a wonder that any of us survived.

VOLTIMAND: These are very extraordinary discrepancies from the story which we heard yesterday. Did you not observe the Prince and Laertes changing rapiers?

FIRST GENTLEMAN: No, certainly not. What advantage could the Prince have gained from that? Both rapiers were bated. He had to use a dagger to stab Laertes and then the King.

VOLTIMAND: But Horatio reported that Laertes himself confessed that his rapier was unbated, and poisoned too.

FIRST GENTLEMAN: I never heard any such confession. Laertes

32

said that he had only half an hour left to live, and that he had been slain by the treacherous weapon in Hamlet's hand—he meant the dagger, of course, which Hamlet had treacherously drawn on him instead of carrying on the fencing-match with the bated swords. Laertes called it a foul practice, as indeed it was, and said that he was dying, and would never recover.

VOLTIMAND: Did you not hear him say that the Queen was poisoned, and that the King was to blame? I must remind you that it appears almost certain that the Queen was poisoned.

FIRST GENTLEMAN: If that was really the case, I think it very probable that the poison was put into the cup by Hamlet when it was first proffered to him. We all noticed that he waved it away, instead of drinking from it himself when the King most generously gave him a magnificent jewel in the cup.

HORATIO: At the risk of being turned out of this Enquiry, I must ask if I may put one question to this witness.

(The Chairman then agreed that Horatio might write down the question, which he himself would put to the witness if he considered it relevant. Horatio then wrote on a paper which he handed to the Chairman).

VOLTIMAND: Yes, that is a reasonable question. Can the witness explain—bearing in mind the evidence we heard yesterday that Prince Hamlet's own wound was very slight, and could not have been self-inflicted—what was the cause of the Prince's own death soon after the others?

FIRST GENTLEMAN: Shortly before the Prince's death, I saw him snatch the cup from which the Queen had previously drunk; he took it from Horatio, who had picked it up. I imagine the Prince drank the rest of the poison in the cup in a final access of madness, and so perished.

VOLTIMAND: You say that you imagine he did so. You did not actually see him drink it?

FIRST GENTLEMAN: No. I would swear to having seen him with the cup in his hand, but I am most anxious to say only what I actually saw. It is, I suppose, possible that the Prince died of heart-failure, rather than from drinking poison. He was panting a good deal during the fencing-match, and his forehead was shining with sweat—the Queen actually had to wipe it for him. He was clearly not in good condition, and his attack of violent mania, coming on top of the physical exertion, might have fatally affected his heart.

VOLTIMAND: Nothing that you saw or heard led you to think that the King and Laertes were engaged in a conspiracy against Prince Hamlet?

FIRST GENTLEMAN: The suggestion is fantastic. It was the King and Laertes who were the victims—and the Queen too, if she did die of poison. The Prince himself was the aggressor throughout. As all the witnesses have agreed, he himself received only a scratch.

VOLTIMAND: The expert evidence on Laertes's wound, and even the King's, was that they were not likely to have caused death in so short a time. Horatio's evidence would account for that; according to him, Laertes—like the Prince—died of poison conveyed on the rapier point, and the King died of that and the poison from the cup.

FIRST GENTLEMAN: I would respectfully remind you that the "expert evidence" was in fact that of a professional soldier with no medical experience, as he himself pointed out. It was obvious to all of us who were actually there that both the King and Laertes died of their wounds. The King was covered in blood; he was stabbed right through the body, and hardly had time to utter a word before he died. He gasped out an appeal, most pathetically, to his

friends to help him, but there was no time to do anything
—he was dead in less than a minute.

(The Chairman then said that in view of this most unprece-
dented conflict of evidence, it would be best to proceed
immediately to hear the stories of all the others who were
present, before enquiring any further into the very serious
allegations which had been made. He would therefore now
call the only female witness to take the stand next, and to
state what her position was and how she came to be present
at the events of 28th August).

LADY-IN-WAITING: I have been a Lady-in-Waiting to Queen
     Gertrude for thirty-one years, ever since her marriage—
     her first marriage, I should say.
VOLTIMAND: In that case these terrible events must have been
     particularly distressing for you, Madam. I am very sorry
     we have to ask you to recall them for this Enquiry.
LADY-IN-WAITING: There is no need to apologize. After what
     we have all been through in the last few months, nothing
     can surprise me. Everything at Court has gone to rack
     and ruin since King Hamlet died.
VOLTIMAND: I am afraid I must remind you that witnesses
     must confine themselves to describing what happened on
     28th August, and must refrain from expressing personal
     opinions.
LADY-IN-WAITING: What nonsense! Everything everybody
     has said so far has been coloured by their personal
     opinions. However, I'm quite ready to tell you what
     happened that day as far as I noticed. I attended the
     Queen to the Great Hall to watch the fencing-match. It
     all started quite cheerfully. The Queen had sent a message
     to the Prince that she wanted him to be reconciled to
     Laertes before the match; I suppose you know there had
     been bitter feeling between them, and one can't blame

Laertes for that in the circumstances. Anyway, the Prince agreed, and he and Laertes had quite a long talk before the match started, and shook hands, and everything seemed to be going well. King Claudius showed us the prize he was going to give to the winner; it was a ring with a really magnificent pearl in it, bigger than any the Queen has. Then the fencing-match started.

VOLTIMAND: Did you notice when the Prince and Laertes scored hits?

LADY-IN-WAITING: I can't say I did. I've had to sit through an awful lot of Court functions in my time; one gets into the habit of not attending very much. The Prince must have scored at some point, though, because the King drank his health and we had those deafening drums and trumpets again. The Queen was very pleased that the Prince was doing so well, I do remember that. She offered him her handkerchief to wipe his forehead, and that was when she drank his health.

VOLTIMAND: Could you see whether the Prince touched the cup before she drank from it?

LADY-IN-WAITING: I wouldn't have seen if he had, the Queen was between me and him.

VOLTIMAND: What happened then?

LADY-IN-WAITING: They went on with the match, but I didn't notice much after that, because just then the Queen began to feel ill, and I was looking after her. I heard her give a gasp, and then she staggered, and I was only just in time to break her fall, and let her down with her shoulders resting against the throne. One of the Switzer guards helped me. She seemed to be suffocating, and I loosened her necklace and her dress, but it was all no use, her colour got worse and worse, I . . .

VOLTIMAND: Bring the Lady a glass of water. Take any time you need to recover, Madam, and please don't distress yourself by recalling these very painful memories. There is no need for you to tell us any more about the Queen's death. I will only ask you if you can remember anything about what else was happening in the Hall at the time?

LADY-IN-WAITING: I don't want a glass of water, thank you. I am quite able to go on. Did I notice anything else? There was a good deal of stamping and shouting—something seemed to have gone wrong with the fencing-match, but I couldn't attend to that.

VOLTIMAND: You did not hear who shouted, or what they said?

LADY-IN-WAITING: There was something about treachery, and poison, and blame; I couldn't say which of them used the words. I didn't really take in what had happened till it was all over, and those two fine-looking young men were both lying there dying.

VOLTIMAND: And King Claudius also.

LADY-IN-WAITING: Yes. But it was naturally the deaths of the young men that affected one most. King Claudius—well, it has been difficult for those of us who served King Hamlet and Queen Gertrude for so many years to get used to the new régime.

VOLTIMAND: Both Prince Hamlet and Laertes were dying when you were able to turn your attention to them?

LADY-IN-WAITING: Yes, but I am glad to tell you that Laertes was able to say before he died that he forgave the Prince his own and his father's death. I did hear that distinctly, and it was a great relief to me. As I said, it was quite natural that Laertes should feel bitter after losing all his family in two such terrible accidents, and I am glad to think that before he died he overcame his resentment. His mother was a great friend of mine, and I have always taken an interest in him and his sister. The Queen was fond of Ophelia, too, she hoped to have her as a daughter-in-law, though latterly that seemed less likely because of the Prince's mental affliction. But the Prince spoke to Laertes in a Christian spirit at the end, too.

VOLTIMAND: You did not see the Prince drink from the poisoned cup?

LADY-IN-WAITING: I don't remember anything like that. He spoke for quite a time after the others were dead, but I thought he was wandering in his mind. He spoke to the Queen, though she was quite dead by then, and he said something about how pale we all looked, and having something to tell us. Horatio was with him, holding him up, and there didn't seem to be anything that the rest of us could do. We were all so stunned.

(The Chairman said that the last witness, though the Court was very grateful to her for giving her evidence so courageously, had not thrown very much more light on the crucial points on which the previous witnesses had differed. He would now adjourn the Court for one hour only, as the morning's proceedings had lasted very late).

Diary
(continued)

I've been a blind pitiful fool. But I've no time to write now—I must get hold of the old Lord before the Court meets again in an hour's time. My letter to him last night couldn't have reached him, and I couldn't find him this morning. Marcellus has gone to search for the Players; the First Player's evidence will be essential now.

Three o'clock. No sign of the old Lord. They must be keeping him hidden till this afternoon's session. How could I have been such an idiot as not to see they had a concerted plan? I still don't see why, or what they have to gain. Nobody now can prove they were parties to the plot, they've only got to say they were as surprised at it as I was, and they'd be in the clear. As they were going to concoct a lot of lies anyway, why not that one? I've got to find out what's behind this. . . . There's the drum, the afternoon session is starting, I must go.

Court of Enquiry Proceedings

Second Day, Second Session

(The Chairman, when summoning the first witness at this session, Osric, the second of the two umpires at the fencing-match, said that he gathered from the witness's interjections during the previous day's hearing that he supported the First Gentleman's statement that Laertes scored against the Prince during the third bout, not after the end of it. The combined evidence of the two umpires must be accepted on that point. On the question of whether there was an exchange of rapiers, and Laertes's alleged statement that he had used an unbated and poisoned rapier, he would ask the witness, who he understood was the nearest person to Laertes throughout, whether he could confirm or deny that Laertes made such a statement).

OSRIC: With the profoundest respect to your Lordship, one does venture to say how immensely, but immensely, one resents the very tasteless and frankly malicious interpretation put yesterday on what should surely have been the sacred utterances of a dying man by a really, let's face it, rather *borné* person obviously quite unused to Court circles. He obviously didn't begin to understand Laertes and all that he'd been through. Not only was Laertes's father murdered and his body treated in an absolutely revolting way, simply dragged all round the Palace, but his funeral was positively done on the cheap, with a No Flowers No Mourning announcement made without even waiting to consult Laertes. And then his sister's funeral, my dear, my Lord I mean, that was done on the cheap too, a most shabby affair, no choir or anything, to say nothing of the quite disgusting incident actually beside the grave, which I must say, mad or not mad, was—well, really, what a way to behave. And all this to happen to Laertes, who was the most splendid . . .

VOLTIMAND: You confirm, then, that Laertes never confessed to being a party to a plot against the Prince?

OSRIC: Of course your Lordship is infallibly correct. I was really trying to explain some of the *nuances* of what happened, too futile of me, I do realize that one must simply stick to the starkest and most banal facts, I do trust your Lordship will forgive me.

VOLTIMAND: You are only required to give plain answers to plain questions. Evidence has been given that the Prince drew a dagger and used it to wound Laertes. Was it agreed that the match should be with rapiers only, or was it to be rapier and dagger?

OSRIC: Might I venture to suggest that your Lordship is confusing the challenge with the wager? I know you must have heard about the bet which the King and Laertes had on the match. The King backed the Prince with a wager of six horses, against six rapiers and poniards put up by Laertes—well, actually, there's no harm in admitting it now poor dear Laertes is dead, put up by me on his behalf. The most ravishing French rapiers they were, Laertes got them for me in Paris, I'd asked him to look out for something really special. The belts and hangers of these ones are simply out of this world, they're so elegant, really some of the very best in my collection, which you probably know is rather famous, simply no one in Denmark has anything to touch it. Of course I knew there was really no risk in letting Laertes back his bet with them, he was a far better

41

swordsman than the Prince, such a stylist. Oh dear, that does sound just the least bit in the world unsporting, doesn't it? And as a matter of fact, it wouldn't have worried me too terribly even if the wager had been lost, because after all, though I don't want to sound vulgar, the wolf isn't exactly howling at my door and I could have sent to Paris to replace the rapiers if they had been lost in the wager.

VOLTIMAND: I must ask you again to answer briefly and to the point. I understand that you confirm that the Prince did use a dagger on Laertes and that it had not been agreed beforehand that both rapiers and daggers should be used for the match?

OSRIC: It was mentioned when I conveyed the challenge to the Prince, but the match was begun with rapiers only.

VOLTIMAND: After the Prince had stabbed Laertes, what was his next action?

OSRIC: He started shouting and screaming in the most peculiar way, and absolutely sprang at the King and simply skewered him—too revolting and savage, it was a perfect massacre.

VOLTIMAND: How did the Prince himself die?

OSRIC: I'm afraid I can't be even the tiniest help about that, I'd already left the hall by then.

VOLTIMAND: But we have evidence that the door had been locked.

OSRIC: Do forgive me for putting your Lordship right—it had been bolted, not locked. It seemed to me that someone really ought to call help, with the Prince stabbing everyone in that maniac way, too appalling, I really felt it was my duty to go and summon the Switzers, so I unbolted the door and went and fetched help, and by the time I came back the Prince was all but dead. I did hear him saying something about the poison working on him, so

I suppose he had killed himself with it, after committing all those ghastly murders.

(The Chairman then called the senior Lord-in-Waiting to the late King Claudius, who had been in attendance during the fencing-match, and asked him to describe it and the events which followed).

OLD LORD: I'm afraid I shan't be much use to you. Have to admit I dropped off at the beginning of the match—we'd been up very late the night before, the King had a wassail party. Must have been two or three before we got to bed. I'm not a young man, you know, I find it very difficult to keep awake the morning after a night like that.

VOLTIMAND: Please describe any part of the events which you did witness.

OLD LORD: What's that?

VOLTIMAND: Did you see or hear anything at all?

OLD LORD: Oh, yes, I was only dozing on and off. The Prince and Laertes were talking a bit at the beginning, I remember that. Then I must have nodded a bit, because the next thing I knew was when they sounded off with a drum and trumpets, the King was drinking a health to celebrate a score, so they must have been fencing for a bit before that. Well, after that I dozed off again for a bit. What finally woke me up was a lot of shouting, and when I really came to and had a look round, blest if Prince Hamlet and Laertes weren't both bleeding from wounds, and the Queen in a fainting-fit, fallen against her throne. She can't actually have been fainting, come to think of it, because then she shouted out something, and then the Prince shouted, and then Laertes chipped in, but I'm afraid I didn't catch much of what they were saying, I don't hear quite as well as I used to.

VOLTIMAND: Did you hear anything of what was said?

OLD LORD: Have to get you to repeat that, I'm afraid; I didn't quite get it.

VOLTIMAND: Never mind. Tell us what happened next.

OLD LORD: That was the really extraordinary part of it. Young Hamlet suddenly rushed at the King and stabbed him. I was flabbergasted. I shouted out something about its being treason, and I tried to get at the Prince to hold him back, but I don't move as quickly as I used to do, and the King had pulled over the table, difficult to get at them past it. By the time I got there it was all over, nothing to be done for the King, or the Queen either.

VOLTIMAND: Did you see the Prince drink from the cup before he died?

OLD LORD: I'll tell you what I saw—I saw that young fellow Horatio with a winecup in his hand, and I thought "These young fellows have no respect for anything; imagine having a drink at a moment like this". And obviously the Prince thought the same as I did, because he took the cup away from Horatio.

VOLTIMAND: But did he drink from it himself?

OLD LORD: Why should he do that? I've just told you, he disapproved of his friend having a swig at such a time, he wouldn't be likely to have one himself. There's been too much carousing going on at Court lately—damned bad for the liver. Sets a bad example, too, I've heard people talk, they get to think the whole country's given to the bottle.

(The Chairman then thanked this witness and said he would not ask any more questions, as the witness had been asleep throughout the fencing-match and had not heard any of the statements made later. The only remaining witnesses were two corporals of the Switzer bodyguard who had been on duty in the hall, and he would now call the first of these. He instructed the witness to say how he came to be on the scene).

FIRST SWITZER: I was on duty, attending His Majesty into the Hall to watch the match.

VOLTIMAND: Where did you stand?

FIRST SWITZER: Right behind the throne, till His Majesty sent me off on a message to the Palace Guard sergeant on duty on the ramparts.

VOLTIMAND: How was that?

FIRST SWITZER: The King wanted a salute fired when he gave the signal to the drum, so he waved to me to go and fix it, so I belted off to the ramparts and told Sergeant Francisco about firing the salute, and he said "What, again!", he said, and . . .

VOLTIMAND: Never mind about that. What happened when you got back to the Hall?

FIRST SWITZER: When I got to the door, I found it was locked from the inside. "That's a funny thing" I said. "I'd better go and tell the Major about this" I said, so I was going down to the Guard-room when I saw there was quite a turn-out going on down below in the courtyard and outside the main gate, there was the English Ambassador just arrived, and the Norwegian contingent that was marching through on the way home from Poland, they'd stopped to fire a salute to the Ambassador. Well, just then a gentleman came running down the steps from the Hall . . .

VOLTIMAND: Which gentleman was that?

FIRST SWITZER: They call him Osric. White as a sheet he was, and calling out "Help!", so I said "What's up?", but then he saw all the to-do in the courtyard so he said to tell them all to come quick, and then he ran back, and I saw the door of the Hall that had been locked before was open, so

I ran in after him, and saw the King dead and all the others.

VOLTIMAND: They were all dead when you got back?

FIRST SWITZER: The Prince wasn't, but he was near it. He just said something about news from England, and voting for Fortinbras. He died about a minute after I got back. Then King Fortinbras and the English Ambassador came in, and a lot of the Norwegians, and by then the Major had formed up, and he started ticking me off because I hadn't been in two places at once, he . . .

VOLTIMAND: That will do. You may stand down. The Second Switzer will now take the stand. Did you remain in the Hall throughout?

SECOND SWITZER: No, Sir. I was on duty by the door with a drum, to give the signal to the trumpeters outside when the King drank a toast; they were to be the signal to the guns on the ramparts, you see. His Majesty had one drink, early on, and I gave it a roll on the drum, and there was a salute.

VOLTIMAND: Could you see the fencing from where you were?

SECOND SWITZER: That's right, Sir.

VOLTIMAND: How did it go?

SECOND SWITZER: There was hits on both sides, and then the gentlemen got rather warm, you might say, and there was a bit of a dust-up.

VOLTIMAND: Did you see what happened to their rapiers?

SECOND SWITZER: There was a bit of tugging and shouldering with them.

VOLTIMAND: You did not see them actually exchanged?

SECOND SWITZER: There could have been a swop—I couldn't rightly say there was or there wasn't.

VOLTIMAND: Did you see Prince Hamlet draw a dagger?

SECOND SWITZER: If he did, I wouldn't have seen it, they were scuffling very close. Could be he used one, but I didn't

46

see it. The King shouted just then, to say the gentlemen were to be separated, and I was just running to do that when the Queen took sick, and I had to give a hand with her, just to prop her up against the throne so the Lady could hold her. Then they were all shouting, but the Prince and Laertes had stopped fighting, so I reckoned I'd better get back to my post with the drum. But then the Prince he shouted out it was treachery and villainy and I don't know what, and the doors were to be locked, and to seek it out, so I ran off to the Guard-room to turn out the Bodyguard and make a search like the Prince said. I knew they could lock themselves into the Hall with the bolts inside the door and be quite safe; it never crossed my mind that the trouble was inside the Hall, I thought I was to make a search outside.

VOLTIMAND: But when Prince Hamlet attacked the King . . .

SECOND SWITZER: I never saw anything of that, the King was as right as rain when I left. Laertes was bleeding a bit, but nothing to signify, and the Queen had come over queer, but there was nothing wrong with His Majesty and nothing to show he was in any danger, else I'd never have left the Hall.

VOLTIMAND: What happened when you got to the Guard-room?

SECOND SWITZER: I started to tell the Major I'd been ordered to make a search, but he said if it was only the Prince that said so, to take no notice, everyone knew he was crazy, and I was wanted for a guard of honour in the courtyard for Prince Fortinbras and the Ambassador.

VOLTIMAND: So you didn't return to the Hall?

SECOND SWITZER: No, Sir, not till they all went up there.

(The Chairman then said that no other evidence would be called, as the servants who had brought in the table and the

47

weapons and the wine before the fencing-match had all left the Hall before the match started. He said that the evidence given at the Enquiry so far was extremely perplexing, as the testimony of most members of the Royal entourage seemed to suggest that Prince Hamlet had killed Laertes and then the King with a dagger in an access of madness, and possibly had even poisoned the Queen too, and might finally have killed himself. This, however, was directly contradicted by the evidence of Horatio, who moreover had made the very grave accusation that the King and Laertes had plotted to kill Prince Hamlet by poison. Horatio would be recalled on the following day and asked if he could adduce any proofs in support of this most serious allegation. The Court would now adjourn).

Diary

(continued)

I'm writing this in a tavern down in the City, waiting for Marcellus. He has found the Players, and he sent me a message to say that he'd bring the First Player here after midnight, though the man was nervous about coming. It seemed safest to see him in this little place in a back street. We can't afford to have him tampered with before we produce him in Court as a witness tomorrow.

They won't be here for another hour. This corner ought to be dim enough, the candle is behind me on a shelf, I shan't be seen. There are some men drinking in the other corner, but I'm out of their sight. I've had no time till now to sit back and think it all out. When that bastard stood up this morning and brought out his lies, one after another, I saw that I mustn't let a word that any of them said escape me. All day I've just been watching and listening, not trying to work out what it all means. Now I'm here by myself, I must think out what their plot is, and what I have to do.

Not all of them are in it. Perhaps only the First Gentleman and Osric. There was nothing definite or damning in the evidence of the others, nothing that completely supported the other side—or our side either. The old Lord was playing it safe—I doubt if he's quite as deaf and sleepy as he makes out; he doesn't want to get involved. Can he possibly be such an ass as to believe I would have sat there quietly tippling with the Prince dying beside me? That could have been part of his old fogey build-up. It's a handicap that I'd never met any of these courtiers till a few weeks ago, it makes it difficult to tell what they're normally like and when they're acting. The other side has a big advantage there, they know all these people well.

The Lady-in-Waiting seemed quite well disposed, even though she was a friend of the Polonius family. She obviously loathed Claudius. There was something she said—what was it? I must fix my mind, I mustn't forget anything. No, none of the rest really noticed much. It's my word against the other two. Osric doesn't count for much. His silliness and spite must have been obvious to everybody, and besides, he didn't seem to want to commit himself altogether. He was very evasive about the fencing-match, he managed to avoid definitely confirming the First Gentleman's lies about the Prince having drawn a dagger to stab Laertes. Voltimand seemed to assume he had confirmed it, but he never actually did.

As a matter of fact, Voltimand has been more impartial than I expected. He's fussy and pompous, but he's reasonably fair. If he had to sum up now, I should think he would say it was not proven either way. If I could be sure he would take that line, it might be wiser to say no more. It isn't going to be easy, now that they have managed to put across this picture of Hamlet as a homicidal maniac, to get them to believe in the justification for all his actions. We can do it, but it won't be easy. "Why don't you let it go?" Marcellus said. He knows what Hamlet really was, but he thinks now Hamlet is dead, it doesn't much matter. He helped find the Players to oblige me, but he thinks it's a waste of time.

Not proven: Hamlet would have thought that as bad as guilty. He wanted his name cleared. He wanted everybody to know about his father's murder. I can't let it go. No, I must get through to what is behind the other side's lies.

How astonishing it is that any unbiased person could believe them for a moment. Everyone at Court must have realized what Claudius really was. When his Gentleman got

50

up and spewed out that stuff about Claudius's generosity and his pathetic appeal to his friends, I could have laughed. Did Cicero feel like that when Caesar suddenly tried to protect Catiline at his trial? If I could speak like Cato, I would soon convince them all that Claudius had to be executed, just as Catiline had to be, if justice was to be done. Claudius was really rather like Catiline—a treacherous murderer, plausible too, and a lecher, as Catiline was, and caring for nobody but himself. I suppose he did love the Queen in his way—but not well enough to risk speaking out to try and save her life when she'd drunk the poison. He just tried to protect himself by pretending she was fainting at the sight of blood. A great bloated sack of greed, that's all Claudius was; and yet this Gentleman of his, whom he'd have squeezed and thrown away without the least compunction if there'd been anything to gain by it, is fighting to defend his memory, although the man himself is in no danger. Why? What's behind it? There must be an answer if I only had the wit to see it.

The potboy in this place looked at me inquisitively as he went by just then. I'd better order a drink, to look normal. Some meat and bread, too—I haven't eaten all day, now I think of it.

Now I must get my brain to work again. That creature of Claudius's, that First Gentleman, what do I know about him? Nothing, really—I'd hardly noticed him till he spoke up at the Enquiry yesterday. I must try and remember if he was really close to Claudius. He was in waiting when the play was acted, I'm pretty sure I remember him there, behind Claudius's chair. And wasn't he—yes, I remember now, he was there when Ophelia insisted on seeing the Queen, and Claudius told him to keep a watch on her, after she'd been raving and singing so wretchedly, I remember seeing him follow her after she wandered out and Claudius dismissed us after her. But he seemed just a cypher, one of Claudius's tools, like

Rosencrantz and Guildenstern, but less important. Though of course he's a permanent member of the Royal Household, not just temporary hangers-on as they were, called in for a special piece of dirty work.

I never even heard this man's name. But if he was just a tool, whose tool is he now? Can Fortinbras—he spoke finely about the Prince just after his death, but he may have changed, or been got at, and be manipulating all this. I don't think it's that, though. After all, it was he who ordered this Enquiry, and we're all being allowed to speak freely. He could suppress the whole thing if he wanted to. It doesn't matter to him who was plotting against whom. Now they're all dead, his own title is unassailable. He just wants to prevent riots, and protecting Claudius's reputation wouldn't do that. He can't have been implicated himself in any way; he was fighting in Poland all July and August—besides, he's the last person Claudius would have taken into his confidence. No, the First Gentleman and Osric must be working for themselves, not for Fortinbras. I'll have to discover why.

Later. Marcellus and Bernardo came, bringing the First Player with them. A strange fellow, with that curly beard and a great booming voice—we had to tell him twice to speak lower, or the men in the other corner would hear what he was saying. He and his troupe have been lying very low since that night they acted at Court, they've been afraid of getting into trouble over the play. It was only when they knew Claudius was dead that they surfaced again. Even now, this man is nervy, he wasn't keen to give evidence. I've had to promise him my father's ring, it's the only thing of any value I've got left. My purse is pretty well empty. Well, it won't matter, once this is over.

After he'd gone, the others and I had a council of war. Bernardo is more and more inclined to reveal the Ghost's appearance. He says things aren't going well, and that would clinch our story. Marcellus is dead against it, he says he won't break his oath in any case, he will refuse to testify, and he's convinced it would only do harm, we shouldn't be believed. "It won't help the Prince, and it may harm you" he said to me. "You're not doing yourself any good by all this, you know. You're making a lot of enemies. You want to watch out for yourself".

I didn't tell him how little I cared about that. I agree with him for other reasons, though. It's not good tactics to tell about the Ghost. I want to make it all sound as practical and down-to-earth as possible. I shall spend the rest of tonight writing out what I have to say tomorrow at the Enquiry. It's got to be as clear and convincing as possible. Why can't I argue like Cato or Cicero? The only thing I can do is to be plain and clear. I won't mention the letter to start with, I'll keep that in reserve. I still think it would be better not to tell the story of the voyage unless it's absolutely essential.

I'll draft the statement now. I shouldn't sleep tonight anyway. I'm back in my room in the Palace now. I can hear the sea, it's turned stormy after that sticky heat yesterday. It must be towards dawn, I've only got a few hours.

Court of Enquiry Proceedings

Third Day, First Session

(The Chairman called Horatio as the first witness. Horatio said that the Chairman had required him yesterday to substantiate his accusation against King Claudius and Laertes of having conspired to kill Prince Hamlet. He was ready to do this now, but in view of the importance of this matter, he asked to be allowed to read a prepared statement. The Chairman agreed to this. He warned all those present that no interruptions would be tolerated. Horatio could be cross-examined later if this proved necessary after he had completed his statement. The Chairman added that he had apprised King Fortinbras of what had passed at yesterday's session, and had been commanded to probe until the truth emerged, no matter how long this took or how much of the personal history of the Royal Family had unavoidably to be discussed in public. He called on Horatio to make his statement).

HORATIO: Prince Hamlet's actions throughout the last few months have been directed towards bringing to light and punishing a terrible crime. The perpetrator of the crime, discovering that Prince Hamlet knew his secret, forestalled the Prince's revenge by plotting to kill him. In the resulting catastrophe, both criminal and avenger perished.

Shortly after I first saw the Prince again, after my return to Denmark in April, the Prince told me that he had learned on irrefutable authority that Claudius had murdered his brother King Hamlet in order to secure his throne and his wife.

(Cries and shouts in Court. The Chairman called for silence, and said that anyone making any interruptions would be removed by the officers of the Court. He instructed the witness to proceed with his statement, while solemnly warning him that the penalties for perjury in so grave a matter would be very severe).

HORATIO: At the time of King Hamlet's death it was announced that he had died of snake-bite, having been stung by a snake when he was asleep in the orchard in the Palace gardens. But Prince Hamlet knew that actually his father had been murdered by Claudius, who poured poison into his brother's ear. The Prince was convinced that it was his duty as a son to avenge this horrible crime. In order to have still further confirmation of Claudius's guilt, the Prince set a trap for him. A company of actors happened to arrive at Court, and he decided to make them act a play which would contain a scene exactly reproducing Claudius's murder of his brother. The Prince instructed the actors how to alter a play already in their repertoire, by introducing some extra speeches and actions, so as to represent the murder committed by Claudius. It was agreed between the Prince and me that we would both watch Claudius carefully during the performance, to see if he showed any signs of confusion and guilt during the murder scene, which would prove that he had a similar crime on his conscience. As all those who were present at the performance could testify, Claudius was in fact extremely alarmed and angered by the scene in question; he shouted to break up the performance, and rushed away in the utmost confusion. This completely confirmed Prince Hamlet's conviction of his uncle's guilt, but it also let Claudius know that the Prince knew about his secret crime, and from then on Claudius plotted to kill his nephew. I can swear from my own observation that Claudius showed a guilty terror when the poisoning was mentioned and shown in the play; and I can produce another witness to corroborate Prince Hamlet's intention of trapping the King by this performance. I ask that the First Player should now be called as a witness.

(The Chairman said that he found himself really incapable of comment at this stage on the astonishing charges against the late King Claudius which they had just heard, and which opened up this Enquiry to far wider and yet graver implications. The grounds for this charge would have to be most strictly examined. As a first step, he agreed to call the witness named by Horatio. He would afterwards ask any other persons who had been present at the theatrical performance mentioned by Horatio to come forward and give evidence about it. The First Gentleman here intimated that he wished to testify about this. The Chairman then called the First Player to take the stand, and asked him whether he could confirm Horatio's statement that the play had been altered to entrap King Claudius).

FIRST PLAYER: It was altered all right, but none of us had the least clue what the Prince was driving at. We wouldn't have touched it with a barge-pole if we'd known it was political. The thing was lethal—we found that out afterwards, all right, but we only arrived here the night before the show, and we were rehearsing right up to the last minute, because of the new lines and business the Prince wanted put in, so we never had a chance to pick up the local gossip, or we'd have refused to put in all those lines about second marriages and so on. We sensed during the show that that bit wasn't going over very big, but up till then we hadn't a notion.

VOLTIMAND: What were the extra passages which you were asked to insert?

FIRST PLAYER: Do you know the play—*The Murder of Gonzago*? No? Well, it's not the world's masterpiece, but it's got some nice little scenes, and it generally goes down pretty well, the way we give it. The plot isn't much—the top roles are an old lord, Gonzago, who's a sick man, and his wife Baptista. You have them on stage talking about how ill he is, and how fond she is of him, and is he going to die, and will she be sorry if he does? It's really a bed-chamber scene—the Prince wanted us to make it in an orchard, I don't know why, it's not in the original script; so we had a plant in a pot to show it was out of doors, though it was much less effective with Gonzago lying on a bench than if he's on a great bed, the way we usually play it. Well then, in the original play there's a popular revolt led by Lucianus, who takes on the job of murder-ing old Gonzago—something like Brutus and Caesar it is. That's how it goes in the original text, but the Prince wanted all that changed. He wanted Baptista to get off with the chief conspirator Lucianus, after Gonzago had been murdered. To give a bit of advance dramatic irony for that, he wrote some lines about second marriages being a bad thing, for Gonzago and Baptista, and we fitted them into the bedchamber scene, the orchard scene as it became. Then the Prince said he wanted Lucianus to poison Gonzago by pouring the stuff into his ear, not his mouth. It seemed funny to us, but the Patron Is Always Right. The Prince did know a bit about the theatre, I will say, more than some; but none of these amateur theorists really know what will actually tell on the stage. Take . . .

VOLTIMAND: These comments are unnecessary. Confine yourself to what actually happened.

FIRST PLAYER: That's exactly what I'm doing; I was just going
to tell you what happened about the dumb-show. We
were talking things over among ourselves at rehearsal,
and the Company all thought this complicated business,
altering the whole idea of the play, would never get
across with just a few extra lines put in like that, so we
settled it to show the whole thing first in a dumb-show as
a curtain-raiser, so that everybody would know where
they were when the play itself started. But we might have
spared our pains, because the Prince wasn't pleased at
all, and the rest of the audience just didn't attend—they
were all whispering with their heads together, the King
and the Queen and that old ass, what was his name? The
Chancellor—Polonius, that's it. I must say, we've hardly
ever played to a stickier audience. You couldn't get a
reaction out of them to start with, and then you got all
too much—stopping the show in the middle like that,
just when the big scene was getting under way. And the
Prince kept putting us out, he tried to be a compère, he
kept chipping in with explanations that didn't fit the play
at all, calling Gonzago a duke, and saying it happened in
Vienna, and that Lucianus was Gonzago's nephew and
poisoned him to get his estate. There's nothing whatever
about that in the original play; Lucianus wasn't supposed
to be any relation, he was the leader of a revolt. The
whole performance was a mess, but you can't blame the
Company—we weren't given a chance.

VOLTIMAND: Did the Prince tell you why he wanted the play
changed in this way?

FIRST PLAYER: He certainly did not. You don't suppose we'd
have touched it if we'd known, do you? I wouldn't have
thought he'd have played us such a trick—he was always

a good friend to the Company. I suppose these great men don't bother about what happens to poor devils like us who get caught up in their affairs.

VOLTIMAND: But you agree that King Claudius appeared particularly upset by the poisoning scene in the play?

FIRST PLAYER: "Upset" is putting it mildly. He stood up and started yelling for the lights to go up, and somebody else shouted for us to stop, and the whole audience rushed away—you'd have thought the place was on fire.

(The witness was then told to stand down, and the First Gentleman was called).

FIRST GENTLEMAN: I wish to start by saying in the strongest possible terms that I utterly repudiate the shocking and baseless accusation against the late King Claudius which we have heard this morning. No genuine evidence whatever has been produced to support this wild and wicked flight of fancy—I use no harsher term, because it is clear that it originated in a mind which we all know to have been unhinged. I have no doubt that Prince Hamlet did concoct this fantastic device over the play, but I utterly deny the interpretation put upon King Claudius's reaction to it. I was present during the performance. We all thought it was very confused and mediocre, and in extremely poor taste, and at one point both the King and the Queen expressed their dissatisfaction, and the King asked the Prince whether he already knew the play and was sure there was nothing offensive about it; but the Prince reassured him, and we all concluded it was simply a feeble melodrama by a third-rate company, until suddenly a new character appeared, and Prince Hamlet pointedly said that he was supposed to be "nephew to the king", although up to then the main character had been described as a duke, not a king. Shortly afterwards, this character was depicted as murdering his uncle, that is, the person who had just been identified by Prince Hamlet himself as the king. Naturally King Claudius was appalled by this open threat of murder from his nephew —we all were. The King broke off the play at once, and left in great displeasure. The Queen was very upset, too. It was altogether a most embarrassing moment.

VOLTIMAND: You deny, then, that the King's emotion was due to a resemblance between the scene in the play and any past action of his own?

FIRST GENTLEMAN: The suggestion is ridiculous. All we have heard is a totally unsupported second-hand statement that the Prince had this fantastic suspicion about his father's death. We have heard no proof that King Hamlet was murdered. We haven't been told what the "irrefutable authority" was from whom the Prince heard about the alleged murder. I have shown that the allegation that King Claudius showed signs of guilt at the play is without foundation.

HORATIO: I can produce documentary evidence that Claudius considered his nephew too dangerous to be left alive. It will confirm that Claudius must have had a guilty secret which the Prince knew.

(At this point a message was handed to the Chairman who, after reading it, said that he would have to adjourn the Court for three hours, after which he would call on Horatio to produce the documentary evidence to which he had just referred).

Diary
(continued)

It is going better, I think. He was clever about Claudius's reaction to the play, he thinks much faster than I can. But they've all now heard the real explanation of the whole business, as I wanted to give it to them at the start. All along, up till now, the Prince's actions have been made to seem inexplicable, capricious—mad, in fact. Now they've seen that he had a reason. And they won't be able to explain away Claudius's letter. It was most fortunate that Hamlet gave it to me that last morning so that I could read it at leisure. I can't hold it back any longer, I had to mention it this morning, with the way things were going. I'll begin with it when I give evidence this afternoon.

What a fantastic fellow that Player is. Only interested in how the play went, and their professional tricks; all the danger and tragedy all round just bounces off him. It made him more convincing as a witness, though. He did well enough. I'll send him my ring, he earned it. After all, why should he care for royal plots and threats? He was right, in a way—it's not so pleasant for the ordinary man who gets caught in a cross-fire between the big guns, specially when they haven't asked for it as Rosencrantz and Guildenstern did. I wish that hadn't got to come out this afternoon, but there's no avoiding it now.

Court of Enquiry Proceedings

Third Day, Second Session

(The Chairman opened the session by saying that he had received a message at the end of the morning session which had made it necessary to alter the order of this afternoon's proceedings. Horatio's evidence would have to be deferred for the present. A communication had been received from the English Ambassador, who had made a discovery which might have some bearing on this Enquiry, and the Ambassador had very kindly agreed to waive his diplomatic immunity and testify in person about this. The Court would therefore of course give precedence to His Excellency, and he would now call upon him to give evidence).

ENGLISH AMBASSADOR: I must start by making it clear that I have no intention of interfering in the internal affairs of Denmark; that would be entirely improper. What I have to say relates only to a commission from the late King of Denmark to the King of England whom I have the honour to represent. This commission was brought to London some weeks ago by two emissaries from the Danish Court, Rosencrantz and Guildenstern. To the very great surprise of the English Court, the commission was a request that the bearers should be instantly executed. As the commission was in due form, and properly sealed, the request which it contained was carried out. But as it appeared somewhat unusual, I was entrusted with the mission of reporting in person to King Claudius that his instructions had been followed. I arrived at

Elsinore just after King Claudius's death, and was therefore unable to report to him as I had been instructed to do. I was made additionally uneasy by a remark by the late Prince's friend Horatio to the effect that King Claudius had never given orders for the execution of Rosencrantz and Guildenstern. At the moment we were all too much preoccupied with the dismal scene before us to give much thought to this; and afterwards there were the funerals to attend, and I had to present my credentials to the new King. But, on thinking over what had been let fall about King Claudius's intentions, I decided that it would be advisable to have a careful examination made of King Claudius's commission, which fortunately I had brought with me, and which I have here.

(The Ambassador then handed a parchment to the Chairman, who asked him whether the examination had detected anything unusual in the commission).

ENGLISH AMBASSADOR: Yes, indeed. The seal, as I have said, was authentic—that is to say, it was undoubtedly the Danish Royal Seal, though certain small differences suggested that it was one used by the late King Hamlet, rather than by King Claudius, whose commissions were sealed with a slightly different signet; but both were authentic. But a careful comparison of the handwriting of the commission with other documents written by King Claudius, by the Chancellor Polonius and by the Danish royal scriveners showed that it was not written by any of them. It was in the official style of handwriting, but with some special characteristics; the expert who examined it said that it appeared to have been written with great care by someone whose normal handwriting was probably somewhat different. It has been compared with a letter in the Royal Archives here, addressed to

63

King Claudius and signed by Prince Hamlet, announcing that he had returned unexpectedly to Denmark; and the expert is in no doubt that the two documents were written by the same person.

VOLTIMAND: Do you mean to say that the commission for the execution of Rosencrantz and Guildenstern was written by Prince Hamlet?

ENGLISH AMBASSADOR: So it appears.

VOLTIMAND: But why should King Claudius have entrusted such a document to the men concerned? It seems most extraordinary.

ENGLISH AMBASSADOR: That is not for me to say. It would not be proper for me to comment on the political situation in Denmark. I felt that the surprising provenance of the document might throw some light on the subject of your Enquiry, and that therefore it was my duty to bring it to your notice, but beyond that it would not be proper for me to go.

(The Chairman then thanked the Ambassador for having so helpfully volunteered this important evidence, and for appearing in person to give it. At this point both Horatio and the First Gentleman asked leave to make statements in connection with this affair. The Chairman gave preference to Horatio, as he had already been asked to speak first that afternoon, but this had been postponed to make way for the English Ambassador's evidence).

HORATIO: The statement that I was going to make anyway concerned the document which the Ambassador produced, and another document for which it was substituted. I can explain the whole story, which I had from Prince Hamlet immediately afterwards. He told me that, before he set the trap of the *Murder of Gonzago* performance which I described this morning, he had learned that Claudius was going to send him to England, ostensibly to negotiate about an indemnity, the payment of which was overdue from England. But the Prince saw that this was only a pretext, and suspected that Claudius meant him never to return from England. His suspicions were confirmed by the fact that Claudius was sending Rosencrantz and Guildenstern with him. These two men had originally been friends of the Prince's; they were fellow-students of his at the University of Wittenberg, where I also knew them. But when they turned up in Elsinore after the marriage of Claudius and Queen Gertrude, the Prince realized that they had become tools of Claudius's, and when he heard that they were to accompany him to England, and were bearers of a sealed commission from Claudius, he was convinced that some plot had been concerted to dispose of him when he arrived in England.

VOLTIMAND: To dispose of him? It was Rosencrantz and Guildenstern themselves who were disposed of.

HORATIO: I'm coming to that. In the ship on the way to England, Prince Hamlet managed to get hold of the sealed commission that Rosencrantz and Guildenstern had been given by Claudius. When he opened it, he found it was a command to the Court of England that he, Prince Hamlet, should be beheaded the moment he arrived in England. I have here the commission itself; you will see that it is in King Claudius's own handwriting.

(The witness handed a document to the Chairman, who examined it and then stated that, as far as he could tell, it had in fact been written by the late King, though expert opinion would have to be taken later about this. He added that the contents of the letter were of a very serious nature indeed. The letter referred to important political considerations affecting both Denmark and England, and also made a number of very grave charges against Prince Hamlet's character and conduct).

FIRST GENTLEMAN: May I ask the Chairman to give details of these charges?

VOLTIMAND: I am very unwilling to mention personal matters which may give pain to the families of persons now dead. However, in view of King Fortinbras's command that nothing should be allowed to stand in the way of discovering the truth, I will reveal the charges mentioned by King Claudius. He said that Prince Hamlet had seduced a young lady of good family, in fact of one of the first families in the country, and that when the young lady's father protested, the Prince had brutally murdered him.

HORATIO: I think everyone present will know who Claudius referred to, and will also know that the first half of the accusation is quite untrue, and that the father's death was an accident, not murder. As the Chairman has revealed half the contents of the letter, I call on him to reveal the other half, giving instructions for the Prince to be beheaded.

VOLTIMAND: It is true that the letter does in fact contain such an order. But I must point out that this letter never in fact reached England, nor did the Prince himself arrive there. We have still had no explanation about that.

HORATIO: The Prince told me that when he discovered this infamous letter from Claudius, he wrote another—the one which the English Ambassador produced this afternoon—and sealed it with his father's seal and left it in place of the original letter. Shortly after that, the next day, in fact, the ship on which they were travelling was attacked by pirates, who took the Prince prisoner, and brought him back to Denmark. He had Claudius's original letter with him, and gave it later to me. The letter makes it quite clear that Claudius was determined to have Prince Hamlet finally silenced—he knew too much.

FIRST GENTLEMAN: May I now claim the right to comment which was offered to us by the Chairman earlier on? I can speak with authority on this question—probably with a good deal more authority than the witness we have just heard, who, in addition to his obvious bias, is clearly quite unfamiliar with the inner workings of the Court of Denmark. After the Prince's maniacal attack on Polonius —and whatever the motive was for that, whether it was the private resentment suggested in the King's letter, or some other reason, it cannot be denied that the Prince did in fact kill Polonius—after this horrible affair, the King summoned a Council, at which I was present, and asked our advice, as his friends, about sending Prince Hamlet to England. We all agreed in advising him that he must not risk his own life, so important to the welfare of the country as a whole, by allowing this homicidal maniac to remain at large in Elsinore. It was therefore agreed by the whole Council that the Prince should be sent to England to be kept in temporary restraint. And here I must add most emphatically that I am sure King Claudius's reference to that in his letter has been misinterpreted—perhaps by a mere misreading of his handwriting. The word which has been read as "beheaded" is no doubt in fact "restrained".

HORATIO: What the letter actually says is that his head is to be struck off with an axe. It's not very likely that that could be misread.

VOLTIMAND: I must ask that witnesses should address their observations to me, not to each other, and should wait till called upon to speak. We have got carried past a point of great importance on which I must ask for clarification.

67

Do you say that the Prince avowed to you that he wrote the substitute letter ordering that Rosencrantz and Guildenstern should be executed?

HORATIO: Yes.

VOLTIMAND: That seems a most ruthless and inexplicable action, especially as I understand these men were actually friends of the Prince.

HORATIO: Former friends. The Prince knew that they were in the plot to have him killed.

VOLTIMAND: Had he any positive evidence that they knew what was in the commission from King Claudius that they carried?

HORATIO: It was fairly certain, from their insolent behaviour to him just before and during the voyage, that they had sided entirely with his enemy Claudius.

VOLTIMAND: That does not answer my question. Do you consider that the Prince was justified, on any unimpeachable grounds, in deliberately ordering the deaths of these two men?

HORATIO: He thought he was altogether justified. They had willingly spied on him for Claudius.

VOLTIMAND: You maintain that that gave him the right to have these men executed?

HORATIO: My opinion on that is not relevant.

VOLTIMAND: I must insist on an answer to my question.

(The witness remained silent, and on being ordered again by the Chairman to reply, said that he declined to give any answer on this point).

VOLTIMAND: I must assume from your refusal to speak that in fact you cannot justify the Prince's action. On the other hand, the letter which you have produced—if, as seems likely, it proves to be authentic—does unambiguously show that King Claudius ordered the Prince to be executed. There is no possibility that, as has been suggested, the terms of the letter can bear another interpretation. I have to say that, on the evidence so far heard, it appears certain that King Claudius and Prince Hamlet were each of them planning the other's destruction. In the case of King Claudius, however reprehensible this plotting may seem, his fears were natural; the Prince had threatened his life through the medium of the play performed before him, and had shown his homicidal tendencies by killing Polonius. Any monarch in King Claudius's place would have felt justified in protecting his own life by imprisoning the person, however highly placed, who had menaced it in this way. Imprisonment, rather than the extreme course indicated in his letter, would have been a wiser and more honourable choice on King Claudius's part and, as we have heard, he had the full support of his Council for such a course. Prince Hamlet, on the other hand, while perhaps justified in the precautions he took to examine King Claudius's letter, showed a ferocity, which his own friend has felt unable to defend, in contriving the deaths of Rosencrantz and Guildenstern. Moreover we have still heard no convincing evidence as to the original cause of the Prince's resentment against King Claudius. The King ordered the Prince's death because he feared the Prince would murder him, and the Prince had given him good cause to fear this. But we still do not know why. We have been told that the Prince believed himself to be avenging his father's murder, but the only evidence as to that which we have heard—the evidence as to King Claudius's reaction to the play—is inconclusive. Unless Horatio can bring any further evidence on this point, this Court will feel bound to conclude that the Prince was a victim of delusions which finally drove him into homicidal mania.

HORATIO: I believe I can produce the further evidence that you want. Can I have time to consider?

(The Chairman agreed to adjourn the proceedings until the following morning. If Horatio were unable to produce any further evidence then, he would close the hearing of evidence and announce his conclusions).

I've ruined everything. I couldn't say I thought he was justified, but I feel as if I'd betrayed him and sided with his
enemies. Even Voltimand now thinks he was cruel, violent,
mad. How can I make them see that, though he did do that, he
was not what they think? I've done nothing but make mis-
takes. They forestall me each time. If I'd been able to produce
Claudius's letter before the English Ambassador spoke, they
need never have known about the other letter—no, that's not
right, the news of Rosencrantz and Guildenstern being executed would have come soon, anyway, and it would have
come out how the order had been given. I told the Prince so,
that morning. He said it wouldn't matter, he'd have finished
his task first. He didn't mind its coming out, he wasn't
ashamed of it. Why should he have been? They were reptiles,
fit to be crushed. He didn't think so at Wittenberg, though—
they were good company then, when we all used to go to the
theatre together. I can see now that they were always rather
malicious, but they seemed amusing then. But Claudius only
had to whistle and they came cringing. It isn't that I mind
what happened to them. I mind his doing it.

I nearly threw my hand in tonight, when Voltimand asked
if I could produce any further evidence. I have made a com-
plete mess of what the Prince asked me to do. Worse, really,
than if I'd held my tongue altogether, and let the whole thing
remain a mystery. I've done nothing but harm. I've failed in
the one thing I could have done for him that he really wanted.
It would have been better if he'd let me drink that poison.

I could have said that he wasn't always responsible for his actions. After he'd seen that terrible ghostly face, I wondered if it had really shaken his reason, although he said he was just going to pretend to be mad; there were times when . . .

No. They all believe he was really mad, but he wouldn't have wanted to be let off like that. The story he wanted me to tell was that he had a purpose and a task. I want that too—I want him to be judged and acquitted, not excused.

What can I do now? The Ghost—but they'd never believe me now. I'm not sure that I believe it myself. We saw something—oh yes, we saw it clearly, I can't forget that. And that freezing cold—it was a cold night, but that piercing chill wasn't normal, not at that time of year. The thing, whatever it was, brought that with it. If it spoke to the Prince, it might speak again. I heard it myself, when we took the oath. If it appeared then to demand vengeance, why not now? The kingdom will never hear the truth now, unless I have help. What sort of help am I invoking? The Prince himself wasn't always sure. I must risk it, though. There is nothing else to turn to. It's nearly midnight—I will go and walk on the battlements. Heaven save me.

Later. Nothing. I must have been desperate, to think I would see anything. I went back to that place at the edge of the cliff where we found Hamlet after he'd seen the Ghost. I went as close to the edge as I could bear, but my vertigo came on. It's sheer down, and the waves were crashing on the rocks at the bottom. That might be the best way for me to go when this is over, better than with a dagger—more sure. Less unpleasant for other people, too. I should simply disappear if I did it that way. It's not as if I had any relations anywhere who would miss me.

I had to pull myself away from the edge this time. I went and waited on the watch-path too, but I only met Bernardo
72

and Marcellus, on guard. Bernardo insists on giving evidence about the Ghost, he has sent to Voltimand to ask to be called tomorrow, so it is out of my hands. He says that as things have gone so badly at the Enquiry, it is the only way to clear the Prince's name. He wasn't bound by an oath, as Marcellus and I were. The Prince asked him to say nothing about the Ghost, but he wasn't there when we were made to swear, after Hamlet himself had seen the Ghost. His evidence won't really help. Marcellus knows more, but he sticks to it that he won't break his oath. "Have you forgotten the way we were told to swear it?" he said. "Don't you know what will come for you if you break an oath like that?" If I do go over that cliff when all this comes to an end, Marcellus will think that I was thrown.

We are both bound to be called as witnesses, though. Shall I break the oath? I was to lose Heaven's grace and mercy when I needed them most if I broke the oath. My own need, though, not his. I'll risk that, if it will help. Whatever I have to do tomorrow, God pardon me, and him.

Morning. I slept, though I didn't expect to. What I wrote last night was like a woman. I started this diary to keep notes for the line to take at the Enquiry, not to whine in.

Court of Enquiry Proceedings

Fourth Day

(The Chairman said that before asking Horatio if he had any further evidence to bring forward, he would call an officer of the Palace Guard who had volunteered to testify. He told the witness to take the stand and identify himself).

BERNARDO: My name is Bernardo. I am a Lieutenant in the Palace Guard. I asked to speak because there was something that several of us saw, last May, that showed the Prince had reason to think his father had been murdered. We didn't know then that that was why it appeared, we thought . . .

VOLTIMAND: Why what appeared? Please explain more clearly what you have to say.

BERNARDO: I'm sorry, Sir. It was like this. Back in May, Captain Marcellus and I were on guard on the ramparts one night, about one o'clock. We were in one of the watch-turrets. It was all very quiet, nothing unusual, no noise. Suddenly there was a figure coming towards us along the watch-path on the battlements.

VOLTIMAND: Could you identify this person?

BERNARDO: It was a man in armour.

VOLTIMAND: Did you challenge him to name himself?

BERNARDO: We challenged it all right. It didn't answer. It walked to the end of the battlements and then it . . . went.

VOLTIMAND: Do you mean that this armed man got away along the battlements, and that you allowed him to escape?

BERNARDO: There's no way out there, it's a blind alley.

VOLTIMAND: But in that case he must have returned along the watch-path.

BERNARDO: It didn't do that either.

VOLTIMAND: Do I understand you to say that this figure simply vanished?

BERNARDO: Yes. It was the same the next night when we saw it again.

VOLTIMAND: You keep referring to this figure as "it". What was it that you actually saw? Did you see no face?

BERNARDO: We saw a face, yes. That was the worst part of it. The helmet was open.

VOLTIMAND: Then you must have seen who it was?

BERNARDO: There was no mistaking that. It was King Hamlet.

VOLTIMAND: King Hamlet! But you said this was in May. The King died in March.

BERNARDO: Yes, Sir.

VOLTIMAND: You positively assert that you saw a person who had died two months before, walking on the battlements here in Elsinore? That it was an apparition, in fact?

BERNARDO: I don't know what it was. I know I saw the face. I'd seen him hundreds of times when I was on duty in the Palace, when he was alive. The face was dreadful, but it was the King.

VOLTIMAND: How was it dreadful? Do you mean ... decaying?

BERNARDO: No, not like that. It was alive—more than alive. It had a hungry seeking look—you could tell there was something it wanted desperately. We knew when we saw it again that we must do something to get it what it wanted. We couldn't bear its misery, it was like dead cold all round us. We told Horatio about it after the second time. He wouldn't believe us at first, he said it was just our imagination, but we made him come and watch with us the third night, and then he saw it too, and charged it

75

to speak, and tell us what it wanted. But it didn't speak. We thought it was going to, but it vanished. We tried to stop it, we even struck at it with our pikes, but there was nothing there, the pikes touched nothing.

VOLTIMAND: This is a most strange and awful narrative. Such apparitions have been reported in the past, and we cannot deny the possibility that it could happen here in Elsinore in our own time. But we must not be credulous either. We must have the fullest confirmation from all those who claim to have seen it. You mentioned another officer of the Palace Guard, Marcellus. Is he present?

(Captain Marcellus was then sent for, but refused to give evidence. He said that he was bound by a solemn and fearful oath, given to a person now dead, not to say anything. Asked whether the dead person was Prince Hamlet, he refused to speak, and when the Chairman asked whether he could at least confirm that he had been present on the occasions mentioned by the previous witness, he again declined speaking. The Chairman then said that if he refused to testify, he would be sent to prison. At this point Horatio intervened to say that he was prepared to give evidence, and that as Marcellus had seen no more than he himself had on the last and most important occasion on which the Ghost appeared, Marcellus's evidence would in any case only duplicate his and Bernardo's, and might therefore be dispensed with).

VOLTIMAND: You are not bound by an oath on this matter?
HORATIO: Yes, I swore the same oath as Marcellus. I am breaking it after much thought, in the interests of truth and justice.
VOLTIMAND: Very well. Do you confirm what Lieutenant Bernardo says?
HORATIO: I was not present the first two times when the Ghost appeared, but I confirm his account of the third time. He

76

himself was not there on the fourth night, which was the vital one. Before I come to that, I must explain that after I myself had seen the Ghost on the third night, I felt certain that the spirit of King Hamlet would speak to his own son the Prince, through it—he would not speak to us. So I sought out the Prince, whom I had not yet seen since we parted in Wittenberg—I didn't want to intrude on his grief for his father's death, so I didn't wait on him when I first got back to Denmark for King Hamlet's funeral. I mention this because I want to make it clear that I myself saw the Ghost before I could have heard from the Prince that he had any suspicions about his father's death. After we had seen the Ghost together, Marcellus, Bernardo and I went to find the Prince, and told him what we had seen. He was naturally very much concerned and moved, and he agreed to watch with us on the ramparts that same night, the fourth since the Ghost had first appeared. He and Marcellus and I kept watch— Bernardo had been called away on duty elsewhere—and not long after midnight the Ghost appeared again. It beckoned to the Prince to follow it away, and though we tried to stop him, he went with the Ghost, and we did not see him again for more than an hour, although we searched all over the Palace for him. We found him at last, in quite a different part of the ramparts, that place where they are built out along the edge of the cliff. When we found him, he was in a state of shock, which was understandable when he revealed that he had just been told by his father's spirit that Claudius had murdered him. The Prince had the truth about Claudius's crime from the most sure of all sources—from the victim himself.

VOLTIMAND: The Prince told you immediately what he had heard?

HORATIO: Not in full. He said that the apparition was really his father's spirit and not a fiend taking that shape, as we had feared. Later he told me the full story of the murder which the Ghost had revealed to him.

VOLTIMAND: You did not yourself hear the Ghost speak about this?

HORATIO: I heard it speak, yes. The Prince asked Marcellus and me to swear not to reveal what we had seen and heard that night, and as we were hesitating, we heard the voice of the Ghost commanding us to swear.

VOLTIMAND: You did not see the Ghost at that time?

HORATIO: No, but we heard the voice distinctly, more than once.

VOLTIMAND: Did it come from the battlements?

HORATIO: No, it came from the rock under our feet.

(Commotion in Court. Cries of "Heaven protect us". A woman in the crowd fainted and was carried out).

VOLTIMAND: This is becoming more and more dreadful. Are we to believe—but we must pursue this enquiry, even in face of the most fantastic and appalling testimony. Is it the case that your account of the Ghost's revelations depends entirely on what Prince Hamlet told you, not on anything that you yourself heard?

HORATIO: I have here the Prince's memorandum book, in which he made a note immediately after the Ghost had left him.

(The memorandum book was handed to the Chairman, who said it contained a somewhat confused entry about smiling villainy in Denmark, but the entry was not dated, and as King Claudius's name did not appear, there was no proof that the Prince meant this comment to apply to his uncle, or that the entry had been made on the occasion described by Horatio).

HORATIO: There's another proof. The Prince said, as soon as we found him, that he might find it necessary later to pretend to be mad, and he made us swear not to reveal that we knew of any cause for this. That showed that he was already planning to avenge his father, and that he'd realized that his knowledge of Claudius's guilt put him in danger.

(The Chairman then said that the new and astounding evidence heard that morning required careful consideration, and that he now proposed to adjourn the Enquiry till the following day. The First Gentleman asked if he might first be permitted to put one question to the last witness. This was agreed).

FIRST GENTLEMAN: Did I understand you to say that the Prince announced his intention to feign madness?
HORATIO: Yes.
FIRST GENTLEMAN: This is a new and very significant piece of evidence, and I am sure that the Chairman and all members of the Royal Household will find it as shocking as I do. King Claudius and the Queen and all of us excused what I can only call Prince Hamlet's appalling behaviour—his public sulkiness about his mother's second marriage, his wild insulting way of talking on all occasions, his dishevelled dress, his idleness, his gloom— because we all believed that he was mentally afflicted, and therefore not responsible for his actions. Even the murder of Polonius was more or less condoned for this reason. But we now learn that all this was feigned—a mere piece of acting, to cover sinister designs. This casts an entirely new light on the whole situation, and I hope the Chairman will view the Prince's actions in this light. I should like to recall that it is not denied that the Prince murdered Polonius, that he in effect murdered Rosen-

79

crantz and Guildenstern, that he stabbed King Claudius to death, that he killed Laertes in an anything but fair fight; and I would add that it is more than probable that he poisoned his own mother Queen Gertrude, and that he was to some extent responsible for the death of Ophelia. And we now learn that this fearful list of crimes was committed, not by a maniac incapable of knowing what he was doing, but by a sane man using a pretended madness to conceal what we now realize must have been a raging and ruthless ambition. The cock-and-bull story which we have been told this morning, about a so-called apparition which none of the witnesses heard say anything to the purpose—if indeed they heard or saw anything at all, which I take leave to doubt—is an entirely unconvincing explanation of the Prince's motives. It will have been noticed that one of the party who concocted this nonsense has subsequently lost his nerve, and refuses to speak in support of it, on the far-fetched excuse of an oath sworn to someone who is not available to confirm it. The whole thing is clearly one lie piled on another. But while he was presenting us with this fairy tale, the last witness accidentally let fall a vital piece of evidence, as to the Prince's plan to pretend to be mad, which has, I hope, provided the final proof needed to bring this Enquiry to an end, with the only possible verdict.

(The Chairman said that it was not proper for any witness to pre-empt the verdict in this way. He had announced that further consideration was needed in view of the new evidence heard that morning, and he therefore ruled that no further witnesses would be called, or allowed to speak, before the Court was adjourned).

Diary

(continued)

I tried to see King Fortinbras. I thought it might help, so I asked for an audience. It was refused, but civilly. I was given a message that he had resolved not to see any of the witnesses till the Enquiry was over, so as to be as unbiased as possible, but that if I applied after the Enquiry was over, my request would be given every consideration. Good enough, I think, so long as it's true that he isn't seeing *any* of the witnesses. The only reason I wanted to see him was to counteract whatever lies the First Gentleman might be filling him up with.

I don't know what to make of this morning's Enquiry. Has it helped or hindered, after all, to tell about the Ghost? Once Bernardo had spoken, I had to break my oath and confirm the story, if only to protect Marcellus. He was furious with me afterwards, of course, he blamed me for breaking the oath and reminded me again how dreadfully we were bidden to swear; and he said it was nonsense to bother about him, he wouldn't have minded going to prison. He said "The trouble with you is, you think because you're called after Horatius that you've got to keep the bridge at all costs. The timbers were being hacked away behind the three of us—it was obviously sensible to run back while we could. I didn't at all like the look of the Tiber". He loves making fun of my admiration for the Romans, and pretending he's disillusioned and cowardly. Actually he's got a religious mind. I remember thinking that when he was talking about Christmas, that night on the ramparts.

There were one or two things at this morning's session that may be to our advantage. The First Gentleman over-reached himself in that last speech of his. Voltimand didn't like being told what verdict he was to give, or having his summing up done for him. I don't believe he's altogether convinced by their account of the fencing-match. He thinks Claudius and Hamlet were each plotting against the other, and he won't have been unduly impressed by that long list of people the Prince is supposed to have killed unprovoked.

The First Gentleman didn't trap me into an involuntary admission, as he thought he had. I brought it out deliberately that the Prince had warned us he was going to pretend to be mad. That ought to have scotched the homicidal mania idea. They must see now that he had a purpose behind what he did. The other side is going to try to make out that his purpose was to get the crown for himself, but that cock won't fight. If that had been his motive, he would only have needed to get Claudius out of the way; he was the acknowledged heir to the throne; why should he have killed Laertes too? He never cared much about being king; only intermittently, anyway.

No, I think the other side is getting rattled, and at any rate Voltimand and the public have now heard the whole of the true story, and the news is bound to spread. How frightened they all were, simply to hear of the Ghost, a shiver seemed to go across the crowd. I expected they would be incredulous, as I was when Marcellus first told me about it. But you could see they believed it, they were so uneasy, crossing themselves and looking over their shoulders. Could anyone else have seen the Ghost at that time? Perhaps there have been rumours. Even Voltimand looked rather queer when I told them about that voice under our feet.

Still it was inconclusive as far as the Enquiry is concerned. What next? I'm still bound to produce some more evidence, to prevent Voltimand from summing up as he said he meant to. There must be some way of showing conclusively that Claudius was in mortal terror lest some secret should escape, and ready to do anything to stop it. I must find something. I'll read back over this diary to see if it reminds me of any . . .

Later. There I was interrupted. A man called Reynaldo has been to see me. He says he was Polonius's steward, and he wanted to see me about what they said at the Enquiry yesterday about Ophelia having been seduced. He said he hadn't wanted to have any truck with a friend of the person who'd killed his old master, but I'd spoken up at the Enquiry to say it wasn't true about Ophelia, and so he'd decided to come to me. It seems that all Polonius's servants are very indignant about the slur on Ophelia, and this man has been trying to get Osric to bring it up again at the Enquiry, and deny the charge, but Osric wouldn't do anything, so Reynaldo came to me. There wasn't a word of truth in it, according to him—she was buried with a virgin's rites, and that was what she was. He acknowledged that she'd said and sung some pretty raw stuff when she was mad, but he swore that wasn't personal, she'd just picked it up from the servants without really knowing what it meant. She'd been left too much to her own company after her mother died; her father was strict, but he was always busy and didn't see much of her, and her brother was away a lot. Then he said something like that it would have been better if Laertes had stayed at home and looked after his father and sister, instead of jaunting off to France and keeping bad company; but when I tried to press him on this, he shut up and wouldn't say any more. It might be worth having him called as a witness at the Enquiry, then he'd have to answer. I did ask him if he wanted to be called so that he himself could speak in Ophelia's defence, but he seemed jumpy at the idea, and said it needed to be someone important at Court, and he asked if I wouldn't speak again. I promised to think it over, anyway, and to see what I could do.

Since then I've been thinking about that poor girl. She was

just a puppet—she said what they told her to say, and let herself be used as a bait in a trap. It's no wonder the Prince was bitter and brutal to her that evening at the play, he knew she'd betrayed him. Perhaps she never really understood what was going on; she wasn't very intelligent. I don't want to drag her name into the Enquiry again if it can do no good. It's a wretched story altogether. She ought to have been better looked after, after Polonius's death, and not allowed to kill herself. I didn't hear how it happened. The inquest must have been while I was at the coast meeting Hamlet when he got back from the voyage. In all that wrangling and shouting at her funeral, nobody said how she actually killed herself, though that priest did say she'd have been buried as a suicide if Claudius hadn't forbidden that. It does seem extraordinary that she wasn't better looked after. I remember thinking so that time when she came raving to the Palace to see the Queen. Why didn't some of those courtiers—that Lady-in-Waiting who gave evidence, for instance; she said she was so fond of Ophelia, and such a friend of her mother's. There was something odd about that woman's evidence, I took a note of it at the time. No, I've just looked back, there's nothing definite. What was it she said? Something about Laertes losing all his family in two accidents. Polonius's death was an accident, all right, it's useful that she made that point. But you could hardly call Ophelia's suicide an accident. I wonder. Is there a possible lead there? Would it be worth while—yes, I think I'll go and see if I can find the Coroner who conducted the inquest on Ophelia. If there's anything there, I could have the Lady-in-Waiting called again as a witness.

Later. So that was it. I see the whole thing now. This should do the trick. I'll have to see Reynaldo again; I've arranged about having the other witnesses called. Better not to put anything more on paper meanwhile.

84

Court of Enquiry Proceedings

Fifth Day, First Session

(The Chairman opened the proceedings by saying that Horatio had requested that the transcript of evidence given at the Coroner's Inquest on Ophelia, daughter of the Chancellor Polonius, should be read to this Enquiry, and that certain witnesses should afterwards be called. It was not apparent what relevance this could have to the present Enquiry, but since Horatio 'had been given leave at a previous hearing to bring forward any further evidence that he could produce in support of the charges he had made against King Claudius, the Chairman had agreed to the proposal. The First Gentleman asked leave to protest, in the name of the late Chancellor's family and friends, at this callous revival of a very sad story which everyone wished charitably to bury in oblivion. His objection was overruled by the Chairman, who then read the following summary of the evidence as to the manner of Ophelia's death which was given at the Inquest on her.

"The Coroner then called on the First Gentleman of the Royal Household to relate what he had seen on the morning of 4th August. The witness said that on 3rd August he had been charged by His Majesty to keep a careful watch on the deceased, who was in an excited and abnormal mental condition, owing to distress at her father's death. He had followed the deceased throughout that day, during which she had wandered about the Palace a good deal and had again intruded on the presence of His Majesty during an audience which he had accorded to her brother Laertes. The witness was again on duty the following morning, to keep a watch on the deceased, but most unhappily she eluded his vigilance and escaped into the Palace garden. When, after searching for her throughout the Palace, he heard that she had been seen in the garden, he hastened to the terrace overlooking the stream that runs through the garden, but was only in time to see the unfortunate young lady run screaming down the opposite bank and fling herself into the stream. She sank at once and did not rise to the surface again. He ran as quickly as possible down the steps from the terrace to the stream, but by the time he got there, some gardeners who had heard the screams had already reached the scene and the body was being brought out of the water. Attempts were made to revive her, but she was quite dead.

Two of the Palace gardeners were then called. They confirmed that they had heard some sounds like singing or shouting when they were working beyond the orchard, and had gone to investigate, and had seen the deceased floating submerged in the stream. They had brought the body out of the water as described".

After the above statement had been read, Horatio asked the Chairman if Queen Gertrude's Lady-in-Waiting could be called, and could be asked if she knew anything about the circumstances of Ophelia's death. The Lady-in-Waiting was summoned to the Enquiry, and the Chairman put the question indicated above).

LADY-IN-WAITING: Well, I don't see what that has to do with your Enquiry, but I'm quite ready to tell you about it, as I actually saw the accident—I was the nearest person there, which makes it all the more horrible that I could do absolutely nothing to save the poor child.

VOLTIMAND: You actually saw her drowning?

LADY-IN-WAITING: Yes. I had gone out into the garden because I'd heard that she was wandering there by herself, and I thought she ought not to be alone. I went on to the terrace to see if I could see her anywhere—you can see most of the gardens from there. I was at the farther end of the terrace, the left-hand one immediately above that pool in the stream where she fell in. The balustrade at the end of the terrace looks almost straight down on to the pool. The trees below the terrace hide the path at the bottom on the near side of the stream, but you can see the pool itself and the other bank. I was looking out over the balustrade when I saw Ophelia come wandering along the opposite bank and climb into the willow-tree which hangs out over the pool. It obviously wasn't safe, specially as she was only holding on with one hand, she had the other full of wild flowers, and she was trying to hang them on the willow-branches, poor dear, I suppose she thought it was her father's tomb. I was just going to call out to her to be careful when she climbed farther out and put one foot on a little rotten branch which couldn't possibly bear her weight, and it broke and she fell straight into the stream.

VOLTIMAND: Fell, not jumped?

LADY-IN-WAITING: Of course not. There was no question of that, it was a pure accident.

VOLTIMAND: But you say that you saw this from some way away. Can you be sure?

LADY-IN-WAITING: Perfectly sure. My sight is very good, and I was immediately above her and could see every detail—the flowers she was carrying, for instance. I remember thinking how surprising it was that she had managed to find *orchis mascula* still in flower at the beginning of August; that's long purples, you know, it normally flowers in May and June. I suppose that cold spell we had in May must have made it flower very late.

VOLTIMAND: May I ask why you did not tell this story, so much at variance with other accounts of Ophelia's death, when the inquest was held on her?

LADY-IN-WAITING: What other accounts? I never heard any. The reason why I didn't volunteer to give evidence was because the First Gentleman of the Royal Household, who also saw the accident, told me it wasn't necessary. I was running down as fast as I could from the terrace to try and save the child after she had fallen in, as she didn't sink at first, but on the way down I met the First Gentleman and he told me that help had already arrived and she was being got out of the water, but he feared it was too late. He said it would only distress me to see the body, there were plenty of people already there helping, and that he had seen the whole thing and would report the accident. I went straight to Queen Gertrude and told her what I'd seen. There can't have been any mistake at the inquest, because the verdict was "Christian burial", and she was buried in the churchyard, though I must say the priest who took the service did seem very disagreeable and perfunctory. Has there been any talk about this? It is extremely unjust if so, as the whole thing was a pure accident, I'm ready to swear that.

(The Chairman then handed to this witness the transcript of the evidence given at the Inquest on Ophelia, and asked her to read it. The First Gentleman asked leave to make a statement. This was agreed).

FIRST GENTLEMAN: I should like to explain that the Lady-in-Waiting is quite correct in what she says about our meeting just after the drowning of Ophelia. I did tell her that I had seen the death too, and I agreed that it was an accident, but that was to spare her feelings and those of Queen Gertrude. I knew how upset they would have been by the truth that Ophelia had deliberately thrown herself in. I need hardly add that our dear friend, who told the Enquiry earlier on that she had been in her present post for over thirty years, probably does not realize that her eyesight is no longer as good as it once was, and that she could not possibly have seen the details which she described at that distance.

LADY-IN-WAITING: This is monstrous. The man is deliberately lying. This stuff that I've just read, the story that he told at the inquest, is a pack of lies, and he is deceiving us again now. If he was on the other terrace as he says he was, he must have seen that she fell in because the branch she was standing on broke, and that she floated for quite a time. It's utterly untrue that she ran down the bank and threw herself in. He must have seen quite clearly from the terrace what happened; I certainly could, whatever he says. Wait a minute, though—how can he have been on the opposite terrace? He was halfway down the steps when I met him, and if he'd been coming down at the same time as me, I'd have seen him opposite me on the way. He must have been down below, and coming up when I met him. He must have been right down by the stream, right beside the pool. I wouldn't have seen him there, the overhanging trees hide the path. I believe he was right there when she fell in—I believe he deliberately let her drown.

(The Chairman said that the movements of these two witnesses were clearly of the greatest importance, and he sent for a plan of the terraces and steps overlooking the stream, on which the Lady-in-Waiting indicated her own position and movements and those of Ophelia and the First Gentleman which she had seen. After examining this, the Chairman said that it revealed some serious discrepancies in the First Gentleman's various statements. If he had witnessed Ophelia's death

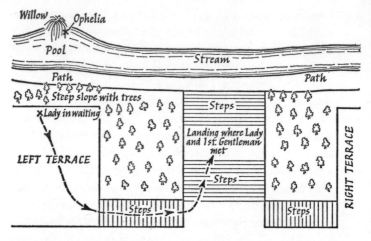

Willow — Ophelia
Pool
Stream
Path   Path
Steep slope with trees
×Lady in waiting
                              Steps
                    Landing where Lady
                    and 1st. Gentleman
LEFT TERRACE   met   RIGHT TERRACE
                              Steps
        Steps   Steps

from the right-hand terrace, as he claimed, he must have been considerably farther away from the pool than the Lady-in-Waiting was, and her view of Ophelia's death was therefore more to be relied on. If he was not on the terrace, but down below by the pool, why had he made no effort to save Ophelia? He asked the First Gentleman if he could give any explanation of his apparently very irresponsible behaviour on this occasion).

FIRST GENTLEMAN: I find myself forced into a very distasteful course of action. Throughout these proceedings I have aimed, as far as was consistent with telling the strict truth, to protect the good name of my late respected master King Claudius. What I have now to say can only cast a slight shade on his memory, without in any way advancing our knowledge of the events with which this Enquiry is supposed to be concerned. When King Claudius charged me to keep a watch on Ophelia, he said at the same time that it was clear that the young lady was hopelessly and permanently beside herself, and that since both her parents were dead and there was no one left to look after her properly, an early death would probably be the most merciful fate that could befall her. I had mentioned to him some of the very wild remarks which she had let fall in her madness, such as that there was trickery abroad in the world, and other strange hints and references which had been overheard by passers-by, and had given rise to most undesirable rumours. King Claudius seemed particularly concerned to hear of this, and appeared to think that Ophelia might have received confidences from Prince Hamlet—about whose fantastic suspicions we have all now heard—and that she might repeat these where they would be overheard. When he ordered me to keep an eye on her, he therefore added that she seemed to be in a violent and even suicidal frame of mind, and that perhaps if she were to take any desperate measures against herself, it would, all things considered, be the truest kindness not to intervene. It was in the light of these royal commands that I refrained from taking any positive action when Ophelia fell into the stream, whether voluntarily or accidentally will never be known for certain. I must add, in defence of my own position, that my instructions from the King had been quite positive; though later, when Queen Gertrude blurted out the story of Ophelia's death before Laertes, just after the King had succeeded in getting Laertes to see reason, the King was extremely displeased with me for not having prevented the death, although he himself had, in a manner, indicated that it would be desirable.

VOLTIMAND: You admit, in fact, that whether or not you acted on instructions, you let Ophelia drown after she had fallen, not thrown herself, into the stream. I must remind you that the evidence which you gave at the Inquest on her was that you saw her throw herself in and that there was no possibility of saving her.

FIRST GENTLEMAN: Here again I was acting under royal instructions. I must point out that there was a great deal of popular unrest at that moment. King Claudius was most anxious that this unrest should be focused on the true cause of all the trouble, that is, on Prince Hamlet, whose criminal actions started the whole chain of events. It was quite clear to all of us at Court that Ophelia's madness was the result of her father's brutal murder, but it was necessary to bring this home to the general public. The news that she had killed herself in despair at her father's death would do this in the most unequivocal way.

LADY-IN-WAITING: I don't understand this. This man's lying again. The inquest verdict was that it was an accident, and that she was to be given Christian burial. He's trying to cover up his own negligence by imaginary instructions from King Claudius.

FIRST GENTLEMAN: I can explain that. The verdict was for Queen Gertrude's benefit. The King didn't want to upset her, so he arranged it so that Ophelia should not be buried as a suicide, since Queen Gertrude would attend the funeral; but the story of the suicide was nevertheless to be promulgated. I can produce evidence in confirmation of this. I demand that the Priest who conducted the funeral service should be called.

(The Priest was then summoned, and the Chairman asked him to tell the Enquiry what instructions he had received about the arrangements for Ophelia's funeral).

PRIEST: The whole affair was scandalous—I may say, sacrilegious. It all seemed straightforward at first. I received word that a funeral service was to be held for a young lady of rank, who had died as the result of an accident. I was told quite positively that, though there had been an inquest, the verdict had been that her death was accidental and that she should be given Christian burial. That was at first. Preparations were therefore made for a full choral service, with wreaths and so on. This was the day before the funeral. Later that day I began to hear a number of rumours from various sources, including even the gravedigger who was employed to prepare Ophelia's grave, that the death had not been an accident, as had been represented to me. The gravedigger went so far as to say that the inquest verdict would have been suicide if the deceased had not been a member of a powerful family. Of course I paid little attention to that, but I thought it my duty to make further enquiries from the Coroner. I then heard that plain evidence of suicide had been given at the Inquest, and that the verdict would have reflected this but for a direct order from the King. Naturally, I then felt bound to say that I could not conduct a regular funeral service for a person guilty of self-murder. It was after this that I received a direct message from King Claudius ordering me to perform the service, which I had perforce to do, though I could not reconcile it with my conscience to say more than the bare minimum of the service, without any sung requiem.

VOLTIMAND: Who brought the message from King Claudius?

PRIEST: It was a young gentleman called Osric. He treated the whole matter with shocking levity, I may say. When I remonstrated at having to give Christian burial to a self-murderer, he said that of course everyone knew the girl had really killed herself, we were just to put a good face on it to keep Queen Gertrude happy. When I said that I should feel compelled to report the matter to my ecclesiastical superiors, he said I could go ahead and tell the whole bench of bishops if I liked, so long as the Queen didn't get to hear about it.

(The Chairman then called Osric, and asked him whether he had carried the message from King Claudius referred to by the Priest).

OSRIC: One really must object to being described as carrying messages, as though one were the second footman. The reverend old boy did come fussing up to the Palace, and I was asked, as a favour, to fend him off, and make it quite clear to him that he was being too ridiculous about the whole thing. We all knew there was this really rather sweet sentimental little plot to keep the poor dear Queen in the dark, but the word had gone round that, apart from that, there was no need to kill ourselves to tell lies about its having been an accident when we all knew it was suicide. And here I do want to make it simply crystal clear that at the time I hadn't the remotest notion that it really was an accident after all, and that I utterly do not hold with having let the poor thing drown like that. I mean, though she was rather a wet girl, let's face it—oh dear, not the best word to have chosen, that, was it? I mean rather a dim girl, but all the same, just to stand on the bank and calmly watch her go under—it does give you a bit of a *frisson* to think of it.

VOLTIMAND: Although the expression is very unsuitable, I must entirely concur with the sentiment. A man who, whatever his instructions, could be guilty of such callous inaction, and could subsequently give perjured evidence about it at a coroner's inquest, has shown himself to be quite unworthy of credit, and all the other evidence he has given so far in this Enquiry must be reconsidered in that light. The story of Ophelia's death and of the Inquest and funeral is so complicated that I had better recapitulate it before we proceed to further enquiries. I un-reservedly accept the account of Ophelia's death given by

94

the Lady-in-Waiting, which showed that the death was an accident, though if Ophelia had been of completely sound mind at the time she would not have risked such an imprudent climb in a tree overhanging a stream. It is also perfectly clear, from the First Gentleman's own later admission, that he gave perjured evidence at the Inquest that he saw her deliberately throw herself in. It also emerged that both the Coroner and the Priest received instructions telling them, in effect, to ignore this false witness, and I should have preferred to believe that King Claudius knew of the First Gentleman's cowardly inactivity, and of the fact that he had perjured himself at the Inquest to protect himself, and therefore King Claudius was taking steps to counteract this and clear Ophelia's reputation. But what are we to think of the widespread rumours that the death was really suicide? No attempt seems to have been made to muzzle the Coroner, or to stop gossip at Court, provided it did not reach the Queen's entourage. On the contrary, if we are to believe the evidence of Osric—and we must not allow its frivolous expression to prejudice us against believing it—the rumours were even deliberately encouraged. And this lends colour to the statement by the First Gentleman, to which I should not otherwise now be inclined to give much credit, that the suicide story was deliberately leaked to the public, in order to damage Prince Hamlet's reputation. This is a very dark affair, and it may be that some criminal proceedings against a certain person will arise out of it. I therefore warn all those present not to leave the Palace premises for the present, nor to hold any communication with each other during the adjournment. The Enquiry will be resumed this afternoon.

Diary

(continued)

It has won our case—but my God what a filthy story. Poor Ophelia, poor wretched child. That woman's account of her with her flowers, thinking she was putting them on her father's tomb—I remember her singing something about that when she was with the Queen. And that man just stood there watching when the branch broke, and let her drown.

He was telling the truth for once when he said that Claudius wanted her dead, and was afraid of what she might let out. I have a horrible feeling that something I said may have helped to put the idea into that man's head, and he may have passed it on to Claudius. I remember I wanted to get the Queen to see her, and I said something about its being dangerous for people to hear her raving. I only said it to frighten the Queen into seeing her, but the First Gentleman may have thought I'd heard Ophelia say something revealing. But then why didn't they try to kill me off too? They thought then that Hamlet was safely on his way to England to be executed, and with Ophelia dead, the only danger would have been if I'd heard something from her. Perhaps they did have something arranged for me, but it was just after that that Laertes burst in with his supporters, and then I got the letter from Hamlet to go and meet him at the coast, and I disappeared for several days. Yes, I expect that was it. Afterwards, when Hamlet himself turned out to be still alive and dangerous, they wouldn't have bothered about me. Claudius himself never really noticed my existence, except once at Ophelia's funeral when he told me to go after Hamlet and keep an eye on him. I suppose Claudius thought I was a cheap edition of Rosen-crantz and Guildenstern. He wouldn't have trusted me, of course—he didn't trust them, either, or anybody; but he probably thought I was too insignificant to be dangerous.

I'm writing this in a room by myself. We've all been put into separate rooms till this afternoon's session, though I don't think Voltimand can have any doubts now about my having told the truth. He wants to keep Osric and the First Gentleman separate. He sees now that they must have con-certed their story, and it looks as if Osric was ready to turn King's evidence, he's losing his nerve, he was very keen to make it clear he knew nothing about how Ophelia really died.

I wanted to have another talk with Reynaldo after what we heard this morning, but I don't think it will be necessary. He was there in Court, and I was watching his face when he heard about Ophelia's death and that man letting her drown. I think he'll tell anything he knows now, without any prompting from me.

Court of Enquiry Proceedings

Fifth Day, Second Session

(The Chairman announced that a new witness had asked to be heard, and called him to take the stand and give his name and occupation).

REYNALDO: My name is Reynaldo. I was Steward to the late Chancellor Polonius. I want to say that I have volunteered to give this evidence, though it won't sound well for my young master, because the world ought to know how he was led astray by that Claudius—him that said my young lady was to be left to drown, and wrote a lot of lies to the King of England about her being no better than she should be, which there's not a word of truth in it. The young master, Laertes, he would never have done what he did without he'd been talked into it by the King. When he came back from France, he was all for demanding justice fair and openly, and you can't blame him for that, the way his father had been murdered. He went straight to the Palace to ask what they'd done to his father, and to say he meant to have his rights. But when he came back, he was different, he'd been talked over. After that he shut himself up, except when he went to my young lady's funeral. He never went out, and he wouldn't see the people that came to say they were ready to support him. He'd been got at, that's what it was, and if he was in any plot, it was King Claudius thought it all up, Laertes was led into it by him, that I'll swear.

VOLTIMAND: This is all opinion and hearsay. Have you any real evidence of a plot?

REYNALDO: There's something I found out when I was in Paris. My old master sent me there with some money for Laertes. That was in June. Polonius told me that as well as handing over the money to Laertes I was to make some enquiries first about how he was behaving, and what sort of a reputation he had there. That was the old master's way—he was always going on about what people would think and say about him and all the family, he thought a good deal of that. Well, I did what he said. I put up at the inn where a lot of Danes stay when they get to Paris, and I got talking with some of them. I made out I was working for the family of a young lady Laertes was to marry, and that the family wanted to know if he was well thought of. I didn't get much, but there was one gentleman that said a funny thing. I asked if Laertes was a friendly gentleman, making out I didn't know him at all, you see; and this other gentleman, he said "Friendly's not the word I'd choose, but I wouldn't get into any fights with him if I were you—he's rather too good a customer of a certain quack". They all laughed then, but they wouldn't say any more, and my old master had told me I was to go about it indirectly, so I didn't like to press the gentleman. But I asked around about this quack doctor they spoke of, that Laertes had dealt with, and after a while I found someone that told me he was a specialist in weapon poisons.

FIRST GENTLEMAN: I demand to be heard. I swear I knew nothing about this. I see now that it must have been true about Laertes's rapier at the fencing-match being poisoned, but I knew nothing whatever about that. Osric was entirely responsible for bringing in the rapiers, and it was he who gave what must have been the poisoned one to Laertes. Whatever plot he and Laertes had against the Prince, King Claudius and I knew nothing about it.

99

OSRIC: He's lying, he's lying. He was in the whole thing. It was all worked out the night before, we actually rehearsed it in the hall, he and the King were there with Laertes, they rehearsed the whole thing and how the special rapier was to be handed to Laertes. I did know about that, I knew it was unbated. I thought that was fair enough, why shouldn't Laertes have given the Prince a scratch or two when the Prince had murdered his father? But I never knew about the poison, I swear I didn't. . . .

FIRST GENTLEMAN: You see, he acknowledges he was part of a conspiracy. I knew nothing about it till now, I absolutely deny it, it's all a lie that the King and I were there the night before. The King hardly saw Laertes after his return from France, just for two brief audiences and the funeral. Laertes was a very untrustworthy subversive person, he tried to organize a revolt against King Claudius and make himself king. It was all a revolutionary plot by him and Osric, King Claudius and I were quite blameless. . . .

OSRIC: Blameless! You knew nothing about it till now, didn't you? Why, you heard Laertes's dying confession, we all heard it, he implicated the King all right, he said it was the King who put poison in the cup, too, and poisoned his own wife. . . .

(At this point the First Gentleman drew a dagger and attacked Osric, whom he slightly wounded before he was disarmed by Captain Marcellus. The Chairman ordered both the First Gentleman and Osric to be removed from the Court and imprisoned to await trial. After order had been restored in Court, the Chairman summed up his conclusions, which on King Fortinbras's orders were later promulgated throughout Denmark as the authoritative version of the late events).

VOLTIMAND: The full truth of this most tragic and terrible

affair has now at last become apparent. Horatio's version of the events has been shown to be the true one, and I congratulate him on his courageous persistence in bringing the truth to light.

In the opening stages of this Enquiry into the deaths of King Claudius, Queen Gertrude, Prince Hamlet and Laertes, a great deal of evidence was given as to how these deaths took place which has since been proved to have been completely untrustworthy, and to have been given by the witnesses concerned in an attempt to disguise their own complicity in an infamous plot. It is now clear that the surviving participants in this plot not only conspired to protect themselves by giving perjured evidence to this Enquiry, but also tried to suppress the true facts by suborning or intimidating other witnesses, and even contrived that King Fortinbras's orders for an autopsy of the corpses should not reach the Court doctor till too late.

In spite of their efforts to pervert and obscure the true story of these events, it has now been conclusively shown that King Claudius plotted the death of Prince Hamlet; first by the commission sent with him to England, ordering that he should be executed; then, when that failed, by conspiring with Laertes and others to contrive the Prince's death by means of a poisoned rapier and a poisoned drink. The fact that he plotted against his nephew to this extent, without ever making any open move against him, proves that the Prince had some real hold over him. This can only have been some guilty secret, otherwise King Claudius could have had the Prince openly tried for Polonius's murder. Obviously Claudius could not risk this, as the Prince would then have revealed the secret which Claudius was prepared to do anything to suppress. We now have separate proof of that; we know that, on the mere suspicion that Ophelia might have been told by Prince Hamlet what Claudius's secret was, Claudius virtually signed Ophelia's death warrant. Claudius dared not allow the Prince, who enjoyed much popular support, to put his case in open court. Claudius therefore arranged for him to be shipped off to England and secretly executed there. When the Prince's vigilance enabled him to escape that danger, Claudius arranged another plot which would make it appear that the Prince had met an accidental death in a fencing-match.

We must now come to the question of what Claudius's guilty secret really was. We have heard, on the evidence of a witness who has now been shown to be trustworthy, that the Prince believed Claudius's secret to be that he had murdered his own brother, King Hamlet, in order to secure the succession to the throne for himself. Two very different categories of evidence as to that have been advanced at this Enquiry. The first was that when a play depicting a murder identical with Claudius's alleged murder of his brother was performed before Claudius, he showed every sign of guilty confusion. This evidence, I am bound to say, is open to more than one interpretation; but it should be borne in mind that the First Player, who was not aware of the undercurrents of that evening's events, agreed that it was the representation of the murder itself that terrified Claudius. The reference to its being a nephew's plot against his royal uncle, which has been suggested as the true cause of Claudius's terror, apparently occurred somewhat earlier in the play, and produced no reaction from Claudius, so the suggestion that he was frightened by what he saw as a threat from his nephew to his own life cannot be sustained.

The second category of evidence that Claudius's secret

was the murder of his brother is far more important—indeed in a sense more sacred—than any conclusions to be drawn from a mere stage performance, but it presents even greater problems. We have been told, on the evidence of two witnesses of credit, that the phantom of the late King Hamlet appeared on the ramparts of the Palace, and one of these witnesses further states that the phantom revealed to Prince Hamlet the horrible secret of his murder by his brother. The description by these two witnesses of the apparition which they saw certainly made a profound impression on all those present at the Enquiry, and it was apparent to us all that they were relating, as truthfully as they knew how, an experience of an altogether exceptional nature. We cannot ignore the possibility—indeed, the probability—that the spectre of the late King Hamlet, who, as all his subjects gratefully remember, devoted his life to the advancement of Denmark's interests, may have appeared to warn his beloved realm that its throne was being usurped by a treacherous murderer.

On the question of Claudius's guilty secret, I therefore conclude that, while the evidence is not totally conclusive, the strong probability is that he was in fact guilty of fratricide—and I fear I must add, of adultery and of incest. These, however, are not the questions which this Enquiry was set up to resolve, though the elucidation of the final events in this tragic process inevitably involved investigation of the secret motives leading up to the tragedy. On the questions which were the specific terms of reference of this Enquiry, I pronounce as follows:

Queen Gertrude died of poison drunk from a cup which was intended for Prince Hamlet.

King Claudius and Laertes died of poison in rapier

wounds given them by Prince Hamlet, but they themselves were responsible for the poison being on the
rapier, and the Prince acted in legitimate self-defence.
Prince Hamlet died of a poisoned rapier wound given
him by Laertes, treacherously from behind when the
Prince was off guard.

I now declare this Enquiry closed.

Diary
(concluded)

Chantry of St. Patrick. I came here to get some peace. Marcellus wanted to organize a party to celebrate the result of the Enquiry, and Voltimand asked me if I would "do him the honour of dining at his house". I said I had to come here to do penance for the oath I broke.

The Brothers will let me stay here for a few days, though I've no money left to pay for my keep. I've still got my ring, though. The First Player wouldn't take it after all, which was decent of him. He made a theatrical scene out of it, of course, with a broken voice and his arm round my shoulder, but still it was good of him.

Fortinbras has sent a message offering me a job at Court as his equerry. I shan't take that, anyway. Soon I shall have to decide what I'm going to do, whether to go on, but not just yet. I'm going to sit here and think.

What Hamlet asked for is done, more or less. Does he know, wherever he is? He asked me to stay in this world and do it; to stay away from the felicity of the other world. I hadn't any doubt then what he meant. He was on the verge of reaching rest, and he thought it would be happy rest, and that I should join him there at last. That's what I thought then that he meant. Now, I don't know; I don't know what he believed. Perhaps he was just suggesting I should wear the statutory Court mourning and not go to parties for a while; that I should not stop missing him and start enjoying life too soon. If he meant that, he should have known me better. I won't believe his last words were as trivial as that. He was asking me to give up something really worth attaining. He must have believed in the peace that he was going to. Though if he heard me say so, he would probably laugh at me and remind me of that stinking skull of Yorick's, and his own father's ghost clinging resentfully to Elsinore and earthly injuries. That's all true. Hamlet's own body is rotting now in his father's marble tomb, and his own shadow could come out of it and walk on the battlements as his father's did. But that's not what matters. Rest, silence, felicity.

This is a good place to pray in. It's quiet and bare. If I do decide to go on, maybe I will stay here for good, and join the Brothers, if they'll have me.

I shall sleep now. The thing is done. Perhaps it wasn't what he most wanted, after all. I never knew if he really, in his heart, cared about vengeance. Some of the time he did, but if he had really wanted it, why did he leave it so long? I sometimes thought I could divine what was in his mind, but I was never sure. No one will ever be sure about that.

NOTE

In what season of the year did the events in *Hamlet* take place? Shakespeare himself obviously never bothered to give this a thought; weather and seasons mattered very much to him, but not the literal time-sequence of his plays. But he scattered some clues in *Hamlet* which can be picked up and assembled by those who enjoy working out this sort of puzzle.

The action of the play, which starts about six weeks after the murder of Hamlet Senior, and about three weeks after the marriage of Claudius and Gertrude and the coronation of Claudius, covers between three and four months. There are a few conflicting indications of the time of year when the events took place.

1. Hamlet Senior was having an outdoor siesta in his orchard when he was murdered. This suggests summer.
2. Six weeks later when his Ghost appeared, it was bitter cold on the ramparts. This frosty night can hardly have been later than May or earlier than October.
3. But it must all the same have been fairly near the shortest night, since the Ghost appeared between twelve and one and the dawn started fairly soon afterwards, which suggests June. Moreover the Ghost mentioned seeing a glow-worm; these are generally seen in late June and July.
4. When, at least three months after the Ghost's appearance, Ophelia went mad and was drowned, she was carrying a bunch of wild flowers which included columbine and long purples (*orchis mascula*), whose flowering time is May to June. Her other flowers—pansies, crow-flowers (butter-

cups), rue, rosemary, fennel, nettles and daisies—could all
have been in flower between late June and September.
5. About two months after the start of the play, Fortinbras
is on his way to campaign against Poland. The summer
was the campaigning season.

The best way to reconcile these indications in a workable
time-sequence seems to be to assume that Hamlet Senior—a
tough athletic monarch—was one of those fresh-air fiends
who sleep out of doors on their balconies even when the snow
lies deep on their sleeping-bags. The afternoon siesta in the
orchard was his "custom *always*". If so, he could have met his
end in March—perhaps during an early warm spell in which
an afternoon sleep out of doors would have been not disagreeable to a hardy man. His Ghost would then have appeared during a frosty spell in early May, when the sun would
be rising about five in the latitude of Elsinore—though I
think the Ghost must have been mistaken in thinking he saw a
glow-worm then. Ophelia's death would then be in early
August. Her columbines and long purples would have been
dead and dry when she picked them, even if the late frost had
delayed their flowering, but she was hardly in a state of mind
to be very observant about this. Her other flowers could have
been still in fresh bloom. Fortinbras's Polish campaign would
have been in July and August.

The last scene of the play would then take place in late
August. I have therefore placed the Court of Enquiry in
early September.